I0590806

STRONG IS HER HOPE

STRONG IS HER HOPE

SCHOOL OF NECESSARY MAGIC BOOK FOUR

JUDITH BERENS   MARTHA CARR   MICHAEL ANDERLE

DISRUPTIVE IMAGINATION

STRONG IS HER HOPE TEAM

Thanks to the JIT Readers

Daniel Weigert
Mary Morris
James Caplan
John Ashmore
Peter Manis
Keith Verret
Larry Omans
Micky Cocker

If we've missed anyone, please let us know!

DEDICATIONS

From Martha

To everyone who still believes in magic
and all the possibilities that holds.
To all the readers who make this
entire ride so much fun.
And to my son, Louie and so many wonderful friends who
remind me all the time of what
really matters and how wonderful
life can be in any given moment.

From Michael

To Family, Friends and
Those Who Love
To Read.
May We All Enjoy Grace
To Live The Life We Are
Called.

I zzie sat alone at one of the long tables in the hall eating her breakfast, listening to the clink her spoon made against the white bowl. No one was back from the Christmas break yet, and Horace had eaten quickly and hurried out to take care of chores.

"Not so easy when you have to do things the old-fashioned way," he had said with a smile, pushing his red curly hair under a plaid wool hat complete with earflaps.

Izzie looked up when she heard a surprised whoop outside and saw Mara Berens flapping her arms, determined to stay upright. Izzie watched as she teetered across the icy sidewalk toward the dining hall.

The headmistress clasped her cold red hands together when she came in, her cheeks rosy from the chill outside. She wore the red knit hat with a pom-pom on top that Izzie had gotten her for Christmas.

"Aren't you leaving soon to go pick up Alison?" asked the headmistress.

Izzie popped the last piece of bacon into her mouth and

nodded. "Mmmhmm, I'm leaving right now. We'll let you know when we get back." *Or at least when we get back to the dorm*, thought Izzie. She had a list of things to do on their way home. Top of the list was visiting the dragon. She'd watched him grow for weeks.

"Okay. Be safe out there, and if you need anything let me know." The headmistress turned to walk away, calling over her shoulder, "And have fun!"

Izzie was surprised but chalked it up to leftover holiday cheer, or maybe the anticipation of a New Year just hours away. *No new memories lately. Maybe it was just a dream I wanted to believe in or bad magic? Let it go. New Year, new chapter.*

She shook it off as she got up from the table and carried her dishes into the kitchen, waving at the pixies hard at work cleaning up the skeleton staff's breakfast.

"Bring Alison by in a few hours, and we'll have something warm for you girls," squeaked Cary, the head cook. Her wings fluttered behind her as she held up a pot five times larger than she was.

"Hot chocolate," chimed Polly, stacking clean dishes on a high shelf. The fat tabby who lived on the grounds, Felix, slipped into the kitchen. He jumped onto the counter, snatched the leftover bacon, and scurried out just as quickly.

"Damn cat!" yelled Cary, throwing a pan that just narrowly missed him.

Izzie waved goodbye, muttering to herself, "Never mess with a pixie." She headed to the foyer and put on her coat and boots. The cold wind slapped her in the face as she stepped outside and marched quickly to the gates to catch the eight o'clock bus downtown.

The jitney was still on the winter break schedule and made no regular stops, but the headmistress had arranged a pickup. The bus was already there waiting for Izzie, and Mrs. Beasley, the bus driver, waved to her through the front window.

Mrs. Beasley opened the stubborn door, which creaked loudly, and welcomed Izzie on board with a kind smile.

"Happy Holidays, Izzie! Nice to see you. You're one of my favorite people."

Izzie smiled. She knew that Mrs. Beasley made a point of saying the same thing to everyone. She also kept butterscotch candies in a pouch that hung by her side and gave them to anyone who looked like they needed a little something extra in their day.

Izzie sat in the front seat of the bus, behind and across from the bus driver.

"Did you have a nice holiday?"

"Oh, dear me, yes." Mrs. Beasley grunted and shoved the long handle, and the door closed with another loud creak. The smile quickly returned to the bus driver's face. "Children and grandchildren showed up in force. It was a full house, I tell you. Thank goodness for magic, or I'd still be cooking." She chortled.

She adjusted her mirror, wiggled her fingers in her fingerless woolen gloves, and drove back toward Charlottesville. "Where to today?"

"I'm headed to the Starbucks to pick up a friend from the train station."

The bus rolled along the country road. Branches heavy

with ice hung low, creating a frozen canopy that the bus drove underneath. Thoroughbred horses ran through a long, wide pasture, warm air streaming out of their nostrils. A woman in knee-high rubber galoshes gave a long whistle, calling them all back to the barn.

Izzie was mesmerized when the horses all turned at the same time, their tails held high as they galloped for the barn.

In town, Christmas decorations still hung from every lamppost and restaurants displayed signs advertising midnight specials for the festivities later that night.

Free Glass Of Champagne with the Meatloaf Special, read one sign. Another advertised that the folk trio the Fleet Foxes would be playing, along with offering black-eyed peas on the menu for good luck, and that they were going to put a silver dime by every plate for good fortune. The latter two were old Southern traditions.

When the jitney passed the local diner, Martin's, Izzie saw people huddling around mugs of hot steaming beverages and chatting with their neighbors or quietly pondering the new day.

"Here we are, Izzie. You need a ride back?" Mrs. Beasley pulled the bus to a neat stop at the curb by the Starbucks and cranked open the door.

"Yes, can you circle back around, please?"

"Not a problem. Have another stop to make anyway. See you in thirty minutes?"

"Thanks, Mrs. Beasley." Izzie jumped off the bus, holding her gloved hand up in a wave as she made a beeline for the door. Her excitement grew the closer she got to the train's platform, which was just through the hidden door.

There weren't as many people as there would be in just a few days. Then students would pour in from every direction, heading to the nearby university or the School of Necessary Magic. Everyone else would get back to their jobs and their usual routines.

Still, it was plenty busy, with townies getting lattes or double espressos and sharing local gossip.

"Excuse me, thank you." Izzie pushed through the crowd and made her way down the hallway and through the magical hidden wall.

She passed through it, emerging on the wide platform at the top of the stairs. Izzie looked over the rail at the intersecting stairs filled with holiday travelers making their respective ways to relatives' houses or friends' parties.

Izzie hurried down the stairs, joining the stream of people. One flight down, she had to step out of the way of a large family as they made their way to another set of stairs to catch a train to Florida.

Fragrant green pine garlands preserved by magic were wrapped around the rails and trailed all the way down to the platform far below. Overhead, Christmas lights sparkled and shimmered. The curved dome was enchanted to look as if snow were falling, although it disappeared just above their heads.

An older witch in a long bright blue woolen coat walked by Izzie, giggling. "It's beautiful in here, isn't it? I always love the holidays." She reached into her purse and pulled out a red-and-white-striped candy cane, handing it to Izzie. "Happy holidays!"

"Thank you!" Izzie replied, smiling.

Izzie filed down the stairs, keeping an eye out for Alison. She was already imagining running to the familiar woods at the school, finding the dragon, and sharing stories.

The train's whistle blew loudly, pulling Izzie's attention back as she peered toward it, careful not to bump into the tall elf in front of her. The bright red train whizzed into the station and stopped on a dime, steam blowing all around it.

"West Coast train arriving from stops in between! Please step back from the tracks. Watch the fingers and toes, at least the ones you want to keep! Allow all passengers to exit before entering. Have your ticket ready," the station manager's voice announced over their heads.

The excitement built in her chest from knowing her best friend was about to step off the train and then a familiar buzz came over her. Izzie looked around, half-expecting to see someone she knew. The feeling came again. It was like she remembered this place from another life. She hadn't told the headmistress, but she had been having lucid dreams at night. Foggy visions of places and people she felt like she knew, but just couldn't place.

The soft needles of the garland gently pricked Izzie's hand as she gripped the railing, waiting for Alison. She was so distracted she didn't notice the dark wizards and witches standing behind the crowd, whispering to each other.

"I tell you, it's her." A young dark wizard pulled his hood up over his head and nudged the witch next to him.

"Impossible. I heard she was dead." The wizard's older

brother shook his head. "All that experimenting with those cheap spells you bought is catching up with you."

The younger wizard scratched his chin and sighed. "I think it's her. Maybe. Sure looks like her. I don't know, you could be right."

"It's been well over a year. We would've heard something. Too many people want to find her. I doubt you and me would be the ones to find her standing alone in the train station like she didn't even know people were after her. We don't have that kind of luck."

"Yeah, maybe… Try a spell just for jollies. See what she does."

"In here? You'll get us arrested. You know the rules." He slapped the younger wizard on the back of his head, frustrated. "I told Mom we shouldn't bring you."

The boy elbowed his brother and glared across the station as his mother, a tall, dark witch with pale ivory skin, glared at them. A deep red cashmere hood covered her dark hair. She gave Izzie a hard nod, signaling her boys to move in closer.

Izzie was still focused on the train, searching all the windows for a glimpse of Alison.

"Is it her?" asked the older son.

"Suspicion without proof is pointless," the mother whispered to her sons, joining them. "For now, we stick to the plan."

Finally, Izzie spotted Alison on the platform looking at all the souls and energy around her. Her white hair hung loosely around her shoulders over a new navy-blue coat James Brownstone had gotten her for Christmas. Alison spotted Izzie and she smiled and waved, but her expression changed from excited to concerned in a flash.

Alison saw the swirl of dark energy hovering near Izzie and started when she realized they were moving toward her friend.

They were tracking her.

"Who is that?" Alison whispered, studying the dark auras that were just a little too close to Izzie.

Izzie noted that Alison's focus shifted behind her, and she whirled around quickly to see the dark witch and wizards. They snickered, and the brothers elbowed each other and pointed at Izzie. The older one shook his hands in the air.

"Boo!" yelled the younger brother. The witch sniffed disdainfully and turned on her heel, heading up the stairs with her toady sons in tow, still snickering.

Izzie rolled her eyes as Alison caught up with her. She wrapped her arms around Izzie and hugged her tightly, sensing the lingering irritation.

"Who were they?" asked Alison.

"Garden-variety magical bozos. Locals, maybe." Izzie shrugged and squeezed Alison, grateful to have her here again.

"Well, who cares about them, because guess what?"

Izzie smiled. "What?"

Alison took her hand as they started up the steps. "It's almost New Year's Eve, your best friend is here with you, and it's one of the most magical times of the year."

"You are so right. I missed you like crazy. I really appreciate you coming back early and spending New Year's with me. Thank goodness your dad said yes!"

"Are you kidding me? I couldn't imagine a better way to spend my New Year's Eve than with my best friend at my home away from home. Besides, I was getting a little bored."

Izzie knew Alison had said that to make her feel better about being alone on the campus during the holidays. "What did you do over Christmas break?"

"I trained some more with Shay in martial arts. I now have a mean roundhouse kick."

"You'll have to show me!"

"Brownstone tried to make an actual Christmas dinner this year. Stuffing, green bean casserole with those little fried onions on top, cranberries...the works. By make, I mean he ordered it and had it delivered."

Izzie laughed as they finally climbed the last set of stairs and walked through the wall into the crowded Starbucks. "That's better than ribs and pizza, right?"

"Oh, we had those too. Dad said it wasn't a holiday without them, and Shay brought the pizza. But yeah, it was really nice. How about you? What did you do with Ms. Berens?"

"We had Christmas dinner, and something called 'spoon bread,' and pickled peaches."

Alison wrinkled her nose, and Izzie laughed. "No, no, it was surprisingly good. Mara brought out an old deck of Oriceran cards and told me stories from her childhood. She said each image reminded her of an adventure. We exchanged presents, and Horace let me ride the stallion. He even made me a leather belt for Christmas."

"That doesn't sound bad at all."

"No, it wasn't bad, but I really wished you and the rest

of our group were here. It was a little too quiet. You know how I like an adventure."

"Even after the last semester? You are an adrenaline junkie."

"Keeps things interesting."

Alison excitedly squeezed Izzie's hand. "How about a gingerbread latte? We're still on break, after all."

Izzie laughed. "When have you ever known me to say no to gingerbread anything?"

The girls ordered and grabbed their drinks and headed out of the Starbucks. Mrs. Beasley and the jitney were waiting at the curb. They climbed aboard and settled into seats.

"This is the start of a really good year. I can just feel it," Izzie declared, but Alison still felt the hovering dark energy that had pulled at her chest ever since the train station. Something wasn't quite right.

2

Whon the jitney arrived at the school's gates, Alison and Izzie hopped off with Alison's bags and the drinks they had gotten at Starbucks.

"Have a happy New Year!" Mrs. Beasley called as she struggled to close the bus's door.

"You too," the girls yelled, waving back.

Izzie smiled. "I didn't realize until now how much I like that lady."

"She's definitely a sweetie, much nicer than the bus driver last year. Remember when he just about blew his top on the way back from our school outing?" The girls giggled.

As soon as they walked through the front doors, the headmistress came out of her office. She looked at them with a big smile. She was carrying a box of New Year's Eve hats and party favors that the girls assumed were for the adults' New Year's Eve party later that night.

"I see you girls got here safely," the headmistress said in a joyful tone. She pulled two sparkly whistles from the box and handed them to the girls. "Go ahead, blow them. It's one of my creations."

The girls glanced at each other and put the whistles in their mouths. When they blew, no loud sound made their ears ache. Instead, magical balloons popped out and floated up to the ceiling. The balloons burst when they reach it and rained magical confetti that disappeared when it hit the floor. Alison watched the energy shimmering all around her and smiled.

"That's really cool!" Izzie exclaimed.

The headmistress put her shoulders back and tilted her head up with pride. "Thank you. I figured it was all the fun of a New Year's celebration without the hassle of cleanup!"

"I'm sure the janitorial staff will thank you for that later." Izzie giggled.

"Where are you girls headed?"

"Right now, we're going up to put my things away," Alison replied. "After that, we're not sure."

"Okay, well, whatever. Have a good time, and don't forget about dinner tonight! Make sure you wear your best dresses. It's New Year's Eve, after all." The headmistress winked at the girls and walked into the dining hall.

Izzie and Alison hurried up the steps. Inside the room, Alison set her things down on her bed and stroked the down comforter. She breathed deeply, taking in the scents of freshly waxed mahogany and the floral detergent they washed the linens in. It smelled just like every other time she had walked into the room after a good cleaning, and it made her feel at home.

"Is it strange that now that I'm here I can finally relax?" Alison asked.

Izzie shrugged. "Not at all. I always feel that way when I move from the headmistress's house back here and everyone else shows up."

The girls concentrated on getting Alison unpacked. She didn't need the help, but Izzie just wanted it to be over with so they could get on to something else.

"What do you want to do? We aren't under anybody's command since school hasn't started yet. We don't have to have permission to do anything, really. I mean, of course, the headmistress likes to keep an eye on me to know that I'm safe, but other than that we are good to do just about anything we want." Izzie sat on the edge of Alison's bed as the girl put away the last of her socks.

Alison turned toward Izzie and smiled, clasping her hands together in front of her. "I figured that since we don't need a pass right now, we could head down to the kemana and do a little shopping. I'm assuming that since the holidays are over and not many of the kids are back from vacation, it won't be that crowded down there."

"I love that idea. I've wanted to go to the kemana all holiday, but the headmistress worried about me being down there by myself, and there wasn't anyone that could go with me."

Alison put her arm through Izzie's and pulled her from the bed. "Well, it looks like we know exactly what we will be doing with our afternoon."

The girls grabbed their jackets and boots and headed down the stairs. The walk to the kemana wasn't too long, but they had no idea what it would be like down there during the holiday season. They crossed the grounds and went down to the steps leading to the underground city.

The shimmering red crystals on the walls lit their way. Alison loved to run her hand down the cool, smooth sides of the stones. She could almost feel their energy surging through her.

When they reached the bottom, they stepped out into the light and Izzie looked around at all the festive decorations. Down the street on the corner was the Café, and the magical coffee cup sign decorated like a Christmas mug caught Izzie's attention.

"We should go to the Café. There's a drink there I want to try." Izzie smiled and grabbed Alison's hand.

Alison laughed. "If you have any more caffeine you'll be up for the next week."

"I don't think it's caffeinated. Yumfuck told me about it. Apparently, it's a drink they serve on Oriceran."

The girls giggled as they ran down the street, dodging between the magical beings. People were taking advantage of the after-Christmas sales, buying clothing for that night's New Year's Eve festivities, or just milling about as they always did. Izzie and Alison dodged to the side as they stepped onto the sidewalk, letting a pair of Kilomea stomp grumpily by.

"I wonder if they ever smile?" Izzie whispered to Alison with a giggle.

Alison shrugged, smiling. "I'm not sure I would want to see that, even if I could."

They were still laughing when they entered the Café. Izzie placed the order. The girl behind the counter smiled and handed them each a Christmas cookie on the house. Izzie put her hand on Alison's, pushing it down back toward her purse.

"I got this one. It's my treat."

Alison giggled. "I won't argue with you."

"So, from what I've been told, when you drink this it kind of messes with the way you interpret colors. I don't know what that's going to mean for you, but it apparently only lasts a minute or two." Izzie smiled and handed her the drink as they made their way back through the crowd to the front door.

"Wow, now I'm really excited to try it."

Outside, Izzie looked around at the magical heaters that created bubbles of warmth around the tables. "Let's relax at a table instead of walking around just yet. The heaters will keep us warm, and we can enjoy people-watching."

"I'm all about it. Whatever we can do to just relax and enjoy our vacation."

The girls sat at one of the round shiny metal tables. They each took a sip, then blinked for a moment.

"Mmm," Alison moaned, swallowing her drink. "This tastes like chocolate, but with a weird fruit mixed into it. I love it. It's like, sweet, but not too sweet."

Izzie nodded, and when she looked around the colors changed right in front of her eyes. She grasped Alison's hand and squeezed tightly. She had to admit it caught her off-guard how strange everything looked when it wasn't the right color.

"Wow. Yumfuck wasn't kidding. The colors *are* different." Izzie looked down at her hands, flipping them over. "My whole body looks green. And you—you look green too. Your hair is this crazy pale shade of shimmering purple. You should definitely think about dying it because it looks amazing on you!"

Alison laughed and shook her head. "I don't know if I'd have the guts to walk around with purple hair. The only person I know who could pull that off is Scarlett. I think that's because she always has crazy-colored hair, or so you all tell me."

Izzie laughed, looking up at a Crystal as it passed them. She leaned toward Alison and nodded at the cold magical being.

"The Crystal looks like a rainbow. Every icicle hanging from its body is a different color. Magical beings are so much more interesting when you add hot pink and yellow to them." Izzie giggled loudly. "Are you seeing anything yet."

Alison blinked as she looked at the passing souls and energy, which were colors they normally weren't. For a moment, it threw her off. She couldn't differentiate between those who were irritated with the crowds and those who were excited to be there.

"Yes, and it's crazy!" Alison glanced around, wanting to sense as much as she possibly could. "It makes it really hard for me to read people or recognize anyone."

"What color is my soul?" Izzie asked, sitting up straight in her chair.

Alison focused her attention on Izzie and smiled. "There are streams of all different colors spiraling through you. It's kind of the way the dragon looked inside his egg."

Izzie smirked. "Oh, watch out. Before you know it, he will have wings and be huge, and be flying over the school breathing fire."

Alison thought it was an interesting and delicious drink. Even though it threw her off, dark magic stayed dark magic. She could still see the swirling black streams that moved through people's souls. Something that powerful and dark couldn't be changed by a simple drink or spell.

Izzie giggled as she watched the people walk past, their skins different colors. "The kemana's normally blue sky is neon orange with pea-green clouds right now. It looks like what I would expect the sky to look like before the apocalypse."

"Let's just be glad it's not that." Alison chuckled and put her drink down.

A minute later, things faded back to their normal hues. Izzie smiled as she looked at all the people enjoying their time in Ruby Falls, running errands and feeling comfortable in their magical community. She thought about her dreams—or nightmares, as she called them at times. They'd started out small, but had grown over time. They seemed so real and vibrant. When she woke up, she didn't know what was memory and what was the dream. One way or another, there was something about her past that she needed to uncover.

She looked at Alison, wanting to tell her about the dreams but stopping. She wasn't sure if it was something she should talk about now, or wait until she had more information.

Alison sat back in her chair and took in a deep breath. "It's really nice to not have anywhere we need to be or anything we have to do. I know it won't last, but being drama-free is amazing, even if it's only for an afternoon."

Izzie decided to enjoy her afternoon with Alison instead of bringing her friend down with her problems.

They had half the school year left. That meant there were still a lot of dreams to be experienced, a lot of information to be found out, and more than enough time to share what had been going on in her head with Alison.

"You're right. It feels like there's always something going on—something beyond what we should be dealing with as high school students, at least in my opinion. Let's just enjoy the day and tackle everything else in the morning."

She knew the world wasn't that simple. There was dark magic everywhere, but while she was still on vacation and had her best friend with her, she was going to enjoy herself.

Slurping their straws made the girls giggle. Izzie took a deep breath and let the last remnants of the drink's effects wash over the scenery in front of her. She glanced at Alison, who was obviously doing the same thing.

"Shall we head down the street? We could check out the different shops."

Alison nodded. "Sounds good to me. There are a couple of shops I want to hit up anyway."

The girls tossed their cups into the trashcan and meandered down the cobblestone streets of Ruby Falls. There were many shops they had never been into, and they figured that since it was a vacation, they might as well check them out.

"This looks like the perfect shop for Aya," Izzie remarked, stopping in front of a porcelain doll shop with magically animated figures in the front window. "It's a doll shop, but I have to admit it's kind of creepy."

Alison giggled as she sensed the energy coming from

inside the window. "I can only imagine, and I really don't want to. I think we'll skip the doll shop today."

"I am not going to argue with you on that one."

They walked past several more shops, deciding to skip them after looking in the windows. There was really nothing they needed, and neither was in the mood to go clothes shopping. They knew they would get their fair share of that when Kathleen came back. As they passed an old bookstore, Izzie grabbed Alison's hand and pulled her back.

"Oh, this is exactly what I was looking for. It's the old bookstore where Peter found that book last year," Izzie said excitedly.

"Yes! I'm in need of some new material to read when I'm awake, and no one else is."

They walked inside. The magical books' energy was enough to allow Alison to make out the probable content.

"Here you go, Alison—a book about witch hairstyles." Izzie laughed. "Apparently, they're from the 50s, 60s, and 70s."

Alison giggled. "Oh, sure. We could make a real statement, you with a bouffant and me with some crazy silver hairstyle."

"Hey, Halloween has always been my favorite time of year."

The girls laughed as they perused the books.

"How about this one? I think it's about romance." Alison smirked, pulling a book off the shelf and holding it up for Izzie to see.

"How to Create the Best Love Spells on the Market," Izzie read out loud, scratching her nose. "I think I'll pass."

"I was thinking more along the lines of buying it for Peter or maybe even Ethan, so he doesn't scream at anyone this year." Alison laughed and put back the book.

Izzie turned quickly around, holding a book close to her chest with a smile on her face. "Everything You Would Ever Want to Know about Gnomes." It's the perfect way to understand our librarian a little bit better. Maybe we could even figure out how to make him like the students better."

Alison laughed and shook her head. "Oh, he's not that bad. You just have to get to know him."

Izzie put the book back and glanced at Alison. "Another thing I think I'll pass on."

Izzie stopped at the spells section and ran her finger down the spine of a bright purple book with shimmering green writing. She pulled it from the shelf and flipped to the first page.

"Hey, this is the book Professor Hudson talked about during class at the beginning of the year. It's all about the different types of magic, and how you can use them to make yourself stronger. Maybe you can help teach me how to control my magic a little bit better."

"It's always worth a try," Alison agreed with a shrug.

"I'm going to get it. Did you pick anything out?"

"Nah. I have my braille reader and an entire library at the school. I'm pretty sure I can find something in there to pass the time. Plus, I think this year is when we can actually check books out and not have Librarian Decker chasing us down the hall."

"Okay, you ready to get out of here?"

"Yeah. Isn't there a jewelry store next door?" Alison asked.

Izzie and Alison walked up to the register where a young and pretty witch stood behind the counter cracking her gum loudly. She looked at the girls and grinned.

The clerk rang up the sale. "That will be seventeen RF, please." She waited as Izzie pulled money from her pouch.

After Izzie paid for the book, the woman wrapped it in gold tissue paper before bagging it and handing it to her.

"Thanks," the clerk said with a smile. "Don't forget about our half-off sale on New Year's Day! There's also a reading that day. The famous wizard Jeffrey Hiligan will be here discussing his time fighting the dark families."

"That sounds interesting." Izzie nodded and glanced at Alison. "I'm pretty sure that tomorrow we'll be getting ready for class, though."

"Bummer," the girl replied, snapping her gum.

The girls left the store and stopped in the front window of the jewelry store Alison had mentioned. Izzie looked at a sparkling silver friendship bracelet in the display. She glanced over and saw Alison reaching for the front door and smirked before following her inside. Each girl went their own way, perusing the merchandise and making purchases.

When it was Izzie's turn at the counter, she pulled out a piece of paper and wrote a note to the cashier, then pointed to the front window. She didn't want Alison to know what she was buying. She actually bought two of them. One she put in her bag, and she held the other tightly in her hand and wandered over by a display of crystal animals on tall shelves along the wall. She found a glass jackrabbit and held it up to the light, admiring the way the light cast different colors along her arm.

Suddenly, a sharp pain passed through her head and she grasped the bracelet in one hand and the glass rabbit in the other, squeezing her eyes shut. She saw the flash of a memory of two people walking in front of her and felt a tug to catch up to them. But just as the woman was about to turn toward her, the memory broke apart and the pain passed.

"Ready?" Izzie opened her eyes and found Alison standing next to her, a smile spreading across her face. Izzie shook her head and carefully replaced the rabbit on the shelf.

"Yeah, sure," she said, doing her best to let it go, feeling the edges of the bracelet in her hand.

They exited the shop and walked across the street to the small park surrounding a large fountain in the center of the kemana.

After the girls sat down, they turned to each other and simultaneously blurted, "I got something for you."

They laughed and handed each other the same exact bracelet. From the shimmering silver chain hung a small charm. The clasp was a troll, similar to Yumfuck, but minus the green tuft of hair.

Alison ran her fingers across the bracelet and smiled. "We'll be friends forever, right?"

Izzie squeezed her hand and held the bracelet on her wrist. "Forever is a long time for magical beings like us so you might get tired of me by then, but forever was what I was hoping for."

Alison giggled. "I promise I will never get tired of you, weirdo."

"I'm going to hold you to that, you know." Izzie laughed.

Alison held Izzie's arm as they strolled down the street toward the next shop and told her earnestly, "You and I are too strange to make many friends and too stubborn to let go of the ones we've made, so you will just have to get used to the idea that I'm not going anywhere. I'm your family forever. No matter what happened in your past, or *my* past, for that matter, saying that someone is my family is extremely important to me."

Izzie swallowed the lump in her throat and grasped Alison's arm tightly, touched by what she had just been told. "I don't know much about having a family since I grew up in an orphanage, but now that I have you as family, I promise you I will never turn my back on you."

Alison took a deep breath and smiled. "Good. Now that that's settled, let's do some more shopping."

The girls laughed and headed to the next shop, which was full of weird and mysterious things. Alison was able to sense the energy of almost everything in that store. Izzie just walked through, wide-eyed at the unusual items on the shelves. There were dark goods like skulls, petrified snakes, and an entire wall of small vials of herbs with no labels on them. In the center of the store was an oblong glass container that hovered two feet above the floor and held thin blue liquid. Izzie walked up to it and stared, watching the liquid bubble and move. There was a silvery film flowing through it.

"If you look long enough, you can see your past, your present, and your future," a voice explained from behind her.

Izzie turned quickly and looked at the old woman—a witch. Her brown hair was streaked with white. Her face was wrinkled and showed the years in the corners of her eyes, and her long broomstick skirt was dirty where it dragged the floor as she walked. Alison stared at the woman's soul, but the woman didn't act like she even noticed. Izzie swallowed hard and turned back to the container, pressing her finger against the surprisingly warm glass. She stared at the swirling silver film, and liquid blue flashes of her dreams flowed through her mind. She almost felt as if she were sinking back into a dream until Alison pulled her hand away from the glass.

"I think we should move on to the next store. I want to get some stuff for Brownstone and Shay."

"Sure," Izzie replied, shaking her head. The old woman was gone.

She glanced back at the container as she followed Alison out of the shop. It was a strange thing to have happened in the middle of the store in the kemana, but she almost wished she had more time. She wanted to see her past—to know what had really happened and where she came from, and figure out who she was.

Alison, on the other hand, had sensed dark magic flowing through the witch and seen the shimmering black and gray energy pulse from the container. When Izzie had put her hand on it, Alison had sensed her energy changing, and it had looked like parts of her soul were draining into the glass. It left Alison with a bad feeling, but she didn't want to alarm Izzie, so she had gently pulled her away. Now she was asking her to help pick out things for her family.

"What do you think about this bracelet for Shay?" Alison asked Izzie running her fingers over the dangling charms. "The shapes are interesting, and it has great energy. Is it pretty?"

"I don't know her very well, but I like it," Izzie replied smiling at the dagger charms hanging from the ropelike chain.

Alison nodded and continued shopping for her dad and Shay. Izzie looked at different items and realized that she had no one to shop for. She had bought the only person she considered family a friendship bracelet, and beyond Headmistress Berens, there was really no one to buy anything for. She shook the sadness off and reminded herself that she would be spending New Year's Eve with her best friend. Everything else could be handled later.

3

On New Year's Eve, Alison and Izzie put on sparkly dresses that came just below their knees, pulled their hair back, and slipped on the matching heels. They might not have a big party to go to with tons of people looking forward to spending the evening with them, but it was a special night.

"What do you think?" Alison asked, twirling. The skirt of her glittering silver dress flowed around her.

"It's beautiful, and it looks like mine." Izzie laughed. "Mine's blue, though, to match my eyes.

"Are your eyes blue? I love blue. I see a lot of blue in people's souls. Sometimes it means sadness, but there are all kinds of different shades."

"I wonder what color eyes my mom had?" Izzie sighed.

Mara Berens and several other of the teachers who had come back early were gathered around a large oak table in the center of the hall. They'd set it up specially for the night, and though the teachers would have an adults-only

New Year's Eve party later that evening, they had invited Izzie and Alison to share dinner with them.

Mara's head was bent close to Eleanor Hudson's and she was shaking her head, saying, "No, no that won't work. I already thought about that idea."

"There must be some way to get the rest of the student body more acclimated to the shifters. I think it would put the parents' minds at ease," said Professor Hudson.

"I agree and when you think of a way to get the shifters to agree to become wolves so that others can stand around and point till they get bored, let me know."

Professor Hudson pressed her lips together and sat back, letting it go for the moment. She was dressed in a long flowing black skirt and a lacy white blouse, with her blonde hair pulled back as usual and her black-rimmed glasses perched on her nose. When the girls walked into the cafeteria, she waved her wand at the ceiling, creating streams of glowing light that gradually changed from one color to another.

"The girls have arrived," Professor Fowler exclaimed excitedly. Her dress was such a bright shade of yellow that Izzie almost had to squint.

Headmistress Berens looked up from her plate and smiled, putting her hands together. "And don't they look amazing!"

"That they do." Professor Hudson looked at them happily.

"Well, come on, ladies, don't be shy. There are two seats reserved between Librarian Decker, who isn't yet here, and a new professor you haven't yet met, Professor Wilson." Mara pointed to the chairs across the table from her, and a pleasant-looking wizard smiled brightly at them.

"Thank you, headmistress." Alison nodded. She was slightly nervous because of all the elder souls near her.

"All right," the headmistress began, standing up and waving her hand over the table. Everyone's glasses filled with champagne except the girls', who got grape juice instead. "It's time for a toast! I…"

Just then Leo Decker, the head librarian, ran into the cafeteria waving a napkin over his head. The red poppy on his bowler hissed and bared its teeth as Leo chased a Willen across the expanse of the room, shaking his other fist. The Willen had run off with a book from the library. It slid the book into the folds of its skin beneath the gray silk vest it wore.

"You sneaky little…"

"Leo!" the headmistress yelled, glancing at the girls.

As Alison watched the energy of the two of them moving quickly across the room, Izzie leaned toward her and whispered a play by play of the action. The girls pressed their heads together and giggled loudly. Even Headmistress Berens smiled, unable to deny that grumpy Leo Decker chasing a Willen across the room with an angry poppy in his hat was one of the funniest things she had seen all year.

After a few moments, Decker finally gave up and grumpily shuffled to the table. The headmistress raised an eyebrow at him and cleared her throat, once again raising her glass.

"I'll keep this short, lest another thief make a break for it through the hall." The girls giggled, and the headmistress winked at them. "So, without further ado, may your New Year's be bright and shining, and may this upcoming year be fruitful, calm, and peaceful for us all."

"Hear, hear!" Everyone clinked their glasses.

As soon as the headmistress sat down, tons of food appeared on the table in front of them. There was turkey, ham, stuffing, bread pudding, and even Jell-O. Everyone dug in, chatting happily amongst themselves.

"Alison, we are really glad to have you with us for New Year's this year. When Izzie told me you would be coming back early, I was touched. You're a very good friend to cut short your vacation at home and spend the rest of your holiday here with Izzie."

"To be honest, I'm really happy to be here with my best friend. I just wish she could've spent Christmas with me. Maybe when things settle down a little bit, we can do that. I know Brownstone and Shay would be happy to have her."

Mara looked at Izzie with worry in her eyes, then back at Alison. She smiled. "That's definitely something we can talk about in the future. But for now, let's all enjoy our New Year's Eve feast and find out what the future will bring us."

As they ate their dinner, Alison and Izzie listened to the professors talking about New Year's fêtes of the past. Professor Hudson took a sip of her wine and wiped her lips.

"When this school had just opened, we used to throw the most amazing parties. The Fixer would show up and everything. The professors would make it a point to be back after Christmas. There were fancy gowns, masquerade parties, and even a magical ball drop one year in the front courtyard."

The headmistress chuckled, swallowing a sip of her champagne. "The ball got out of hand, hit the ground, and rolled all the way to the forest. It was a good thing it was magic since it ran right over Ms. Brunswick, our old librarian."

Everyone laughed loudly at the memory. Alison and Izzie just grinned at each other, feeling like they had been granted access to some secret part of the professors' lives.

"This Jell-O is amazing," Izzie whispered to Alison. "It tastes like whatever flavor pops into your mind."

"Let's hope you're not thinking about Brussels sprouts." Alison giggled.

Izzie stopped the spoon halfway to her mouth and wrinkled her nose before putting the spoon down and pushing the dish back. The plate disappeared, and in its place, a small and intricately-designed popper appeared. Izzie picked hers up and examined it before looking at the headmistress, who smiled and leaned toward the girls.

"They are magical fortune poppers. Pull that little tab, and you will find a surprise followed by your fortune. Don't take too long reading them though. The message will disappear."

The librarian smiled for once and picked his up. He pulled the tab and laughed as a bird flew up out of the top, whistling a tune before it turned into a puff of smoke. He leaned toward the girls and nodded. "We love these. The headmistress creates them every year."

"I've been doing it since my daughter was little," the headmistress added, wiggling her eyebrows.

Neither Alison nor Izzie had ever seen anything like it before, and Alison was excited to find out her fortune. She pulled the tab and watched the magical bird's energy fly around the room. She ran her fingers over the thin piece of paper and discovered it was written in braille.

Darkness will not prevail.

After she read the message it quickly disappeared from the paper, which erupted into a burst of light like the bird had. Izzie looked over just in time to see the message before it disappeared and smiled to herself, knowing that was exactly the message that Alison needed to hear.

"Neat." Alison smiled.

Izzie pulled the tab of her popper and watched a beautiful cardinal, the mascot of the school, rise up, fly wildly in a circle over her head, and disappear into a burst of light. Just as so many other whimsical spells did, the bird made Izzie smile. Without thinking and still smiling to herself, Izzie picked up the fortune and read it, expecting nothing more than you would find at a Chinese restaurant.

You are surrounded by loved ones, seen and unseen.

Izzie's eyes glistened, and she read the fortune two more times before it shimmered and burst into light. She quickly wiped a tear from her cheek and bit the inside of her lip to try to quell her emotions. It was hard, though. She wanted a family so badly, a mother and a father to love her like Brownstone and Shay loved Alison. She wanted that encouragement, those hugs, the arguments between a teenager and her parents, and everything else that went along with having a family of her own.

Headmistress Berens, who sat across the table from Izzie, had read the message on her fortune—something she hadn't even thought to expect. She instantly felt a pang of regret and wondered if she could have done more to help Izzie stay with her mother and father.

Visions of the night they had arrived at the school came into her mind and stirred up her guilt. Their lives were in danger. *Izzie's* life was in danger. In the short amount of time they'd had and with the kind of people who were chasing them, there'd been only one real choice, no matter how much they had all wanted something different. Izzie's life was the only thing that mattered.

When dinner was done, Alison and Izzie went up to the common area in their dorm to have hot chocolate, sit by the fireplace, and play some cards while they waited for the celebration of the new year. Music and laughter drifted up from the cafeteria where those teachers who had come back early danced, drank, and had a little fun before all the students returned.

Izzie reached over to the side table and grabbed her phone checking the time.

"Oh, it's almost midnight. We should get going."

"Yeah," Alison replied. "We want to find Horace before the new year rings in."

"I'm surprised he's not at the party." Izzie giggled. "Not that I blame him."

Alison chuckled. "Yeah, I don't think he's really a magical party kind of guy."

The girls bundled up in their coats and boots and headed out for a walk just before midnight. They crept past the hall, Izzie staring with bugged-out eyes as Professor Fowler did some sort of interesting dance move on the floor. It took everything they had not to laugh as Izzie gave Alison a detailed description.

"Imagine if you flapped your arms, which were bent at the elbows, and moved your feet really fast back and forth, then spun around," Izzie whispered. The girls covered their mouths and raced out of the mansion, closing the doors before bursting into laughter.

"That must have been amazing," Alison squealed, holding her stomach.

"Oh, my God," Izzie wheezed. "I can't even... No wonder we weren't invited."

They stood there laughing for several minutes before finally calming down. Izzie slid her arm into Alison's and squeezed her hand. "Let's go make our own happy New Year before we get pulled into a time warp and end up on Soul Train, magic style."

It was cold, but the sky was clear, and the stars sparkled brightly overhead. The girls clung tightly to each other, shivering and trying not to slip down the icy hills. Alison saw the energy of the small magical creatures in the woods waiting for the winter to end. For Alison, it was a light show.

They made their way to Horace's cabin, where they found him sitting by a welcoming fire with a golden retriever next to him. Horace looked incredibly happy, happier than they had seen him in a long time. The dog sat on the cold ground, a smile on his furry jaws as Horace ran his hand over his head. There was a small plate with a half-eaten sausage in the snow next to him, and a bowl of water as well.

"You girls back already?" Horace smiled.

"Well, you know that I've been here the whole time, but Alison came back to spend New Year's with me."

"Well, then it's our lucky evening." Horace chuckled.

Alison sat down in a chair while Izzie patted the dog on the top of the head. "Where did he come from?"

Horace looked down at the dog and smiled. "He was a stray, I suppose. He found me, and I decided to keep him. He's a good dog, very loyal. It starts to get lonely around here after everybody leaves, even with all the creatures creeping around in the woods."

"Why aren't you at the party? You are missing some serious dance moves." Alison giggled.

"You must have caught a glimpse of Professor Fowler. Yeah, she's a dancing queen…in her own world."

Izzie smiled and watched the dog, feeling something different radiating from him. The dog turned his head and opened his mouth when Horace was about to stick his fork in a piece of sausage. It shot out from underneath and went right into the dog's mouth. Izzie raised an eyebrow, wondering if she were the only one who had noticed. It seemed like the dog knew what was going to happen just before it took place. From the look on Horace's face she didn't think he had noticed, so she decided to keep it to herself.

"It looks like you have a visitor." Horace nodded toward the forest.

From the edge of the woods, two small beady eyes stared at the three humans and the dog sitting around the bright fire. The sounds of Izzie's and Alison's voices had brought the dragon to them.

"Dorvu!" Izzie smiled, stood up, and waved the dragon over.

"I thought I heard you," Dorvu exclaimed happily as he ran over to them.

He stopped at Izzie's feet and looked at the dog, letting out a not-very-serious roar. In return, the dog barked and growled just a bit. Alison laughed, stood up, and walked away from the warmth of the fire for just a moment to greet their not-so-small scaly dragon friend. Izzie hadn't seen Dorvu during the winter break, and she wondered where exactly he'd been. Of course, he was a dragon and prone to mischief, so it might only be a matter of time until she found out.

"We missed you!" Alison told him, rubbing her hand over the dragon's scales.

"I missed you too. It's been really quiet out here since all the students went away. I kind of like it, but at the same time I miss my family."

"I know exactly how you feel," Izzie replied.

The girls rubbed the dragon's belly for a while and made sure he was okay.

"Do you want to come and sit with us by the fire?" Izzie asked.

Dorvu shook his large head. "I'm not a big fan of hot fires."

Izzie thought that was strange, him being a dragon and all, but she patted his head and walked back to the fire. Alison smiled down at the dragon's vibrant soul, rubbed his belly for a couple more seconds, and joined the others.

Dorvu waved his large paw at Horace and disappeared into the woods.

"I've been watching out for him, but most days he's out hunting. You would be amazed by how much food a young dragon can eat." Horace shoved another piece of sausage in his mouth and fed the rest to the dog.

He wiped his hands on his work pants and glanced at the sky. Without the lights from the mansion, the constellations were perfectly visible. He groaned as he pulled himself to his feet and walked to his house, where a brown satchel sat on the wooden porch.

"I brought some fireworks. I figured it would be a nice show for New Year's Eve, and I'm pretty sure the teachers are going to come out and join us."

Izzie smiled and rubbed her hands together. "I love it when you do fireworks with the teachers. They are absolutely amazing, especially when you do the ones that chase down the other students. Of course, since Alison and I are the only ones here, you can skip that this year."

Horace chuckled, looking up as the teachers walked over the hill bundled up in their winter wear, wands out and ready for magic. Horace lined up the fireworks on the snow-covered ground. Izzie raised an eyebrow, wondering how in the world they'd go off if they were stuck in the snow.

The retriever whined and ran over to stand next to Izzie, letting her pet his head. It seemed that she still had a way with animals.

When all the fireworks were lined up perfectly, Headmistress Berens stepped forward.

"All right, who's ready for the show?"

Everyone cheered and lined up next to the headmistress with their wands and elven powers at the ready. They shot their magic through the air, sending shimmering lights blasting toward the fireworks. The fuses caught and started to spark, seemingly protected from the cold of the ground by the magic.

"This is gonna be loud," Izzie predicted, grabbing Alison's arm and grimacing.

"Yeah, but so worth it," Alison exclaimed.

The fireworks shot into the air and exploded brilliantly one at a time. Shimmering plumes of purple and silver crackled in the sky before creating a rain of golden sparks that drifted carefully down into the fields before vanishing. It was the new year, and there was no better way than to mark the beginning of it.

Izzie reached over and squeezed Alison's hand.

"Happy New Year, Alison."

Alison smiled and looked at her friend. "Happy New Year, Izzie."

4

Everyone had returned to school, excited to be back with their friends but bummed to start classes again. That was how it always seemed to work. Everyone was excited to come back from summer vacation, but when they had to return halfway through the year, nobody really wanted to come back. Nonetheless, everyone was talking excitedly as they compared what they'd received for Christmas and discussed what they'd done for New Year's.

"All right, everyone, make your way to the hall. We've prepared a banquet!" Professor Hudson shooed everyone toward the warm foyer.

There was a big dinner in the hall, a celebration to welcome the students back and send forth good wishes and will for the coming spring.

"I love how they do that," one of the students whispered to her friend as they walked into the cafeteria. "They always magically enchant the ceiling. And look at tonight's! It's the night sky, but whatever direction you move, it moves with you."

"I know, it's so cool! And look no matter what corner of the cafeteria you are in you can see every single one of the constellations, including the second moon of Oriceran. I always wanted to see the second moon, and I don't even have to travel through the gates."

Kathleen, Emma, Aya, Ethan, Peter, Luke, Izzie, and Alison sat around their normal table, staring at the platters of roast beef and bowls of mashed potatoes that had appeared. Izzie excitedly piled some of each on her plate and decided it was the perfect dinner for the night. For some reason, she thought this was her favorite meal.

"I love roast beef and mashed potatoes," Izzie exclaimed not paying any attention to the others.

As she placed a piece of roast beef on her plate, she froze and stared down at the food as if it were a foreign object. *Wait a minute. What am I talking about?*

She wondered how she could have come up with roast beef and mashed potatoes as being her favorite meal when she couldn't remember ever eating them before she'd come to the school. They looked great and smelled wonderful, and she could almost taste them before even taking a bite, but she had zero memory of ever eating them before she'd arrived at SNM. The only thing she could think of was that they had been served at the orphanage a long time ago, and though the memory hadn't stuck with her, the sensory information had.

"My mom used to make this when I was little," Emma said happily. "Now, she's a vegetarian, so we don't get anything like this anymore. I did try some of her tofu turkey for Thanksgiving, but ended up going back to the regular turkey that my dad insisted we make."

Izzie laughed and continued putting food on her plate and passing the dishes around, not truly believing that her memory was poor. Moments like these had become far too frequent in Izzie's life for her to simply ignore as if an absent mind were to blame.

At that moment, though, there wasn't anything she could do about it. It wasn't like she could go to Headmistress Berens and explain that she'd mistaken her favorite food without looking like she was losing her mind. Instead of worrying about it she dug into the food, savoring every bite as she listened to the others talk about their winter vacations.

"My parents actually stayed home this Christmas," Kathleen said, poking her mashed potatoes. She was annoyed that she hadn't been able to pick her own food. "At first, I thought I would be upset with no maid service, turndown service, or chef to prepare my food, but in the end, it was actually very nice. My mother even cooked a Christmas ham for us to eat, something I've never seen her do before."

Aya smirked and took a bite of her roast beef. "That sounds really nice, Kathleen. We stayed home too, but my mom didn't cook. My grandma came over and took care of it. It's this thing that goes on between my family members. About ten years ago my mom tried to cook Christmas dinner for everyone, but the night ended with tears, a fire, and my grandmother being bitter as hell about not having her Christmas ham. Now she cooks Christmas dinner every single year and doesn't even let my mother into the kitchen. Secretly, I think my mother loves it."

Kathleen laughed. "I know *I* would love that if somebody said 'Hey, you don't have to cook Christmas dinner for the rest of time.'"

Peter pulled a small box out of his bookbag and set it on the table, grabbing everyone's attention. The group watched as he pressed the button and the sides retracted, allowing a small rotor to come out on top, creating a drone of sorts. He moved the joystick in his lap, which was connected to a computer that controlled the drone.

"This is one of my new creations for the Entrepreneur Club." Peter smiled. "It's a drone that can fly long distances and retrieve things that would normally take people a very long time to collect."

Ethan narrowed his eyes and tilted his head. "Can't you already buy those in the human world at like, just about every electronics place?"

"You can, but they wouldn't be magically enhanced like this one is. You see, this drone is spelled to be capable of picking up extraordinarily heavy objects that range from large animals like elephants, rhinos, and giraffes to houses and cars."

"What would we use it for?" Kathleen asked.

"Think about rescue operations—times when we need to get to people or animals but are incapable of doing so because of floods, storms, fires, and other things like that. You can fly this drone in and pick up an entire ship full of people or a house right out of the flood, or keep an airplane in the air until it makes a safe landing."

"That's pretty cool, but I'd really like to know how you tested it," Ethan replied with a smirk.

"Let's just say that I'm grounded for the rest of my life."

Everyone laughed as Peter grimaced, thinking about

how much trouble he had gotten in for lifting his father's Mercedes out of the driveway and accidentally placing it on the roof of the house.

"Oh? What happened?" Ethan asked.

Peter shrugged his shoulders. "Let's just say that my father definitely won't be allowing me to drive his Mercedes when I turn sixteen."

"Ouch." Ethan grimaced. "It's all right, we can spell a broom for you, and you can ride that."

Ethan laughed along with everybody, but his expression changed as Grace approached the table carrying a blueprint in her hands. She opened it and set it down between Peter and Ethan, smiling.

"I think I fixed our problem from last year. You know, the problem we were having with the phones?"

Peter looked at the blueprint and nodded. "*Nice.* This will definitely fix the issue. Have you tried it yet?"

"Not yet. I figured it was something we could all work on together since it was a group idea. I'm going to bring it to the club meeting and present it to everyone at one time. I figured that way everyone could look at it and point out any mistakes I might have made that I couldn't see."

Ethan was about to comment when Eleanor Hudson stood up at the front and swished her wand, piping a harmonious melody through the cafeteria. Knowing the signal quite well, everyone quieted down as Headmistress Berens took the stage. She pressed her glowing hand to her throat and cleared it before speaking to the entire cafeteria.

"First, welcome back, everyone! I hope you had a wonderful Christmas and an exciting New Year's. We're moving on to the second half of the year, a time for learning, celebrating the changing of the seasons, and focusing in on those last few courses you all need to do well in before the end of the year. For some, it will be the last semester of their career in high school, an end to start a new beginning."

The headmistress looked at the crowd smiling at everyone and nodding as the seniors clapped and yelled loudly. When she continued, her voice was a bit more serious. "The rules you were told about at the start of the year are still in place, the curfew at night and a request that all students stay in town or on school property during the weekends. If anyone spots any suspicious activity, please do not hesitate to come directly to any teacher right away and let us know. Other than that, I wish everyone a wonderful second semester. I'll see you all at the bonfire, which will begin directly after the banquet."

Glimmering sparks shot up in front of every place setting in the cafeteria. After the sparks faded a popper appeared, just like the one on New Year's Eve. Everyone picked theirs up excitedly and eagerly pulled the tab as they exited the cafeteria. Paper birds fluttered around and whistled wildly before fading away in a burst of light. Students read their fortunes aloud, gasping at them and wondering what exactly they meant for their future.

Never fear the dark. It's always a precursor to the light.

A grapefruit a day will keep the mosquitoes away.

When you're feeling weak, think of what always makes you the strongest.

Each fortune had been magically created for the person. It had been debated for years whether they actually told a person's fortune or if they were no more specific than a fortune cookie at a Chinese restaurant.

Ethan pulled the tab on his. A small sparrow flew out, whistling wildly as it dove toward his head, circled his hair, and burst into light. Everyone laughed hysterically at the look on his face as he swatted at the paper bird. His forehead furrowed, his eyebrows pressed together, and redness stained his cheek when he heard Grace giggling across the room. He snatched up the slip of paper and read it out loud.

Often you will fall short, but in jokes you will prevail.

"Do you know what that means?" Ethan laughed. "That means my April Fool's Day joke will be just as badass as last year's."

"Oh, boy," Kathleen replied, rolling her eyes and sighing.

"That's right." Ethan nodded mischievously. "Fear it. That's all I have to say about that. Fear the first of April."

Everyone else read theirs out loud as well, talking excitedly about how close they were to their lives.

"Your style and mindset will take you to the top," Kathleen read with a smile.

"Sometimes it's hard, but being yourself is the best option," Emma read, nodding. "That's exactly right!"

"Love will last forever, especially for you," Aya read with blushing cheeks.

Alison opened hers and got the same message she had on New Year's Eve. She looked up to find Headmistress Berens' energy pushing toward her to let her know it had been deliberate.

Izzie reached out to grab hers, but stopped and pulled

her hand back. When it came down to it, she wasn't really sure she wanted to know what her future was going to bring, especially since she was sure as heck having a difficult time figuring out her past.

"Personally, I love the fortunes. My father used to do them every year at Christmas. It never failed that mine had something to do with fashion or becoming a famous witch." Kathleen smiled adjusting the cuffs of her white button-up shirt over the wrists of her sweater.

Aya shrugged. "I think they're cool, but I don't put any faith in them. You can find meaning in just about any fortune if you believe it has to do with you. Our minds naturally do that. They form a connection with the things that we want to believe."

Kathleen wrinkled her nose and sighed. "Well, aren't *you* a little Debbie Downer!"

The girls giggled at Kathleen's response. Izzie held her popper in her hand, unsure she wanted to open it. She stuck it in her top dresser drawer and pulled on her sweater, making sure she'd be warm enough out by the bonfire. Sure, the fire would be huge, and there would be s'mores, but she knew just how hot it was to stand around the bonfire for too long. She didn't want to get too cold when she stepped back from it.

"I think Aya is right," Alison replied. "To a certain extent, we make our own futures. Of course, other people are able to affect them, but all in all, we shape our lives into what we want them to be. Anytime we read a fortune, we automatically relate it positively to ourselves. At the same time, though, I think there is something to be said for that. I think motivation is key to shaping your future, and that's usually what a fortune does. It motivates you toward the things you're good at or something you want."

"Man, you guys really took that one deep." Kathleen chuckled.

Everyone laughed, lightening the mood a bit. Alison looked at her friends' souls, spotting nothing she hadn't seen before. She was comforted by having them near. When the girls were done getting ready, they headed into the common area and watched the other girls run back and forth, talking loudly and trying to get ready for the bonfire. There was a general air of excitement. Everyone was happy to be back with friends and starting off the year with one of their favorite social events. For the group, though, it was a reason to spend time together, talk about the things they hadn't been able to discuss with their families, and get back into the groove of being in school.

Alison and Izzie had already been there for a couple of days, but having the rest of them back made everything complete. They were pretty sure the school meant a little bit more to them than it did to the others, because they'd found a family and a connection there that they had either lost or never had.

5

Out in the fields beyond the school, far enough away to keep the flames contained, Horace, along with several of the teachers, had put their talents together and created a special bonfire. It was enormous, and magical at its base. It produced a lot of heat, but no smoke. With the surrounding forest so close and so many magical beings making homes there, the professors made sure the fire was unable to burn outside its magical circle. The snow covering the grass was relatively light, and it sparkled next to the fire. It was a clear night sky, the moon large and bright, the stars shimmering, and the constellations almost leaping from the sky. The gnomes stood off to the side, close enough to take in the heat but far enough away to give the students their privacy.

Leo Decker snickered, and his poppy did the same as he stared at the sky. "I miss the sight of the two moons. The two radiant, sparkling moons of my home planet."

The gnomes around him, with their slick bald heads covered in bowler hats, scarves around their necks, and knit gloves on their small hands, nodded and grumbled to each other.

"Agreed," one of the gnomes replied. "I miss the snow too—the way it made everything just perfect. Nobody complained. We all knew it was just nature's way."

"Exactly," the librarian replied. "Earthlings just want an excuse to complain about everything, and you never can trust them—at least not fully. No matter what anybody says, they don't understand magical beings. They keep their distance, which is exactly what I like."

Off in the distance, howls floated on the breeze, the shifters' signature sound. Luke's gaze snapped to Elias Hodges, who was staring intently at him. He gave him a look to let him know that he needed to stay human. Luke pouted. He missed running with the guys he'd met here at school, but at the same time, he was content to stay by Izzie's side since he'd been away from her for the entire winter vacation.

Izzie noticed the communication between Elias and Luke but acted like she didn't, figuring it was none of her business. He'd tell her if he wanted her to know.

"It's a beautiful night, isn't it?" Izzie commented, squeezing Luke's hand and turning toward the fire. "One of the most beautiful winter nights I've seen so far."

"It *is* gorgeous. It reminds me of the time my mother and I went for a run in Alaska, which had some of the most beautiful scenery I've ever seen. We should go there some-time. I think you would like it."

"That sounds like quite an adventure, and you know me...I'm all about an adventure." Izzie laughed.

Luke chuckled and pulled her closer, rubbing his hands

up and down her arms. "You definitely are, which explains why you're with me."

Among the trees across the fields, the faeries danced. Their bright lights flickered in the chilly night air, and they hummed sweetly.

At the edge of the secluded part of the forest, Dorvu stayed in the shadows and listened to the voices of the girls around the fire. His exceptional hearing allowed him to pick them out, even from that distance and in the center of a large number of voices. Kathleen and Aya looked at each other with wide eyes when they spotted the dragon at the edge of the trees.

"Uh-oh," Aya whispered, hoping Dorvu could hear her. "Dorvu, don't let them see you."

They couldn't allow anyone from the school, including the teachers, to find out he was still on the grounds.

Aya gripped Kathleen's wrist and looked around before slowly pulling her away from the group. "We need to lead him deeper into the woods. He doesn't understand that not everyone is going to be as nice as we are."

Kathleen rolled her eyes and let out a sigh. "Fine, but he has got to learn to stay in the woods. Otherwise, they'll probably send him back to Oriceran, and he doesn't know that place even if he's from there."

"I know." Aya sighed. "When he gets a little bit older, we'll be able to explain it to him better. I'm pretty sure he gets it, though. He talks just like us."

They quickly snuck off to rescue their friend, and they lured the dragon back into the woods by throwing marsh-mallows as far as they could into the trees.

"I'm sorry," Dorvu apologized. "I heard your voices and saw the fire. I was just curious."

"I know," Aya replied patting him on the head. "You just have to be really careful. We don't want anyone finding out you're here, or at least not yet. It might not be safe for you."

Kathleen sighed and handed Dorvu the rest of the marshmallows. "Here, you can have part of the party. I'm sorry you can't come with us."

Dorvu sniffed the bag and swished his tail. "Thanks! Human food is the best. Well, next to freshly-caught rabbit."

The girls grimaced, and Aya patted his head one last time. "We'll come visit you soon, okay? We have to get back before somebody notices we're gone."

The girls made their way quietly to the edge of the forest, peeked out to make sure nobody was watching them, and hurried across the field to rejoin the party. Kathleen sighed as they walked, and Aya looked behind her.

"I swear that dragon is going to get us into trouble," Kathleen grumbled, wiping the mud from the side of her pants.

Aya smiled and shrugged her shoulders. "I don't mind it so much. We are his caretakers even when it's annoying, and even if it puts us in danger of getting into trouble. He's too cute to turn away anyway."

Kathleen scoffed. "Try me."

At the right side of the bonfire, standing right on the edge of the heat, was a cluster of students from wealthier dark families who attended the School of Necessary Magic. The school had a reputation for offering one of the best magical educations in the country. It drew people from all over with different levels of magical ability and different opinions on the moral use of magic on Earth. These students were part of the legacy of dark magic. Some came from prominent dark families known to have infiltrated both the government on earth and on Oriceran, and some were the children of those dark wizards and witches who chose to stay out of the limelight until they were called upon.

The group was known for causing problems. Even during a large school event meant to be fun and exciting and bring them together with others, they stood together making jokes about the other students and set off small magical bombs, laughing as the kids jumped back and almost fell into the large fire.

"Did you see that one kid? He almost became a roasted pig." One of the dark kids laughed, elbowing his friend.

"Watch this one," his friend replied. He twisted his wand and sent out a ball of magic that bounced from student to student until finally finding a home in front of a small group of freshmen. It hovered for a moment, then exploded, scaring the hell out of the kids.

"Good one." They laughed, high-fiving the guy. "Talk about pissant freshmen. I bet they couldn't do our parents' kind of magic if they were held at wand point."

"*Pfft*. They probably can't even tie their own shoes."

They chuckled to each other, adjusting their Mark Jacobs button-up shirts, Calvin Klein dress pants, and imported black dress coats. On their wrists, they all wore either Rolex watches, gifts from their rich family members, or in the girls' cases, Tiffany bracelets with heart charms.

Headmistress Berens watched as they teased and

taunted the other students, irritated that behavior like that was accepted by their parents. She lifted her hand and flicked her wrist to send out a ball of fire that whizzed into the center of their group and hovered for a moment before exploding. All of them jumped back, startled by the sound, and shoved their wands into the inside pockets of their jackets.

They glanced at her as she gave them a menacing look, then turned back sullenly, muttering among themselves that the headmistress could expect grievances to be filed.

"Pathetic Light Elf-witch hybrid. She only got this job because she's related to Leira Berens, and I won't *even* get into *that* bullshit."

Headmistress Berens heard their mutters. She could punish them for talking about their headmistress that way, but she was trying to keep the peace with the dark families —something she couldn't do if she constantly dragged their kids to detention. Instead, she turned away from them and looked at the other students, reminding herself exactly why she was doing what she was doing.

It's the best for everyone, Mara. Just stick to the plan.

She had dealt with that type of bullying for years. The dark families wanted to be in control of the schools, so they attacked her, but she never let it get to her, nor would she let them take control. The most important qualities of the school were its safety, security, and the fact that it was free of the practice of dark magic. So far, she had done a pretty good job keeping the school intact.

Headmistress Berens turned her attention to Izzie and her group, who were standing on the other side of the fire. They watched the dark families kids stewing in their own displeasure and shaking their heads when they didn't get their way. Izzie had seen the headmistress toss the fireball into the group. She chuckled and leaned into Kathleen.

"There's trouble. More of their kind are getting admitted every year."

Kathleen rolled her eyes and shook her head. "One of them magically short-sheeted my bed at the beginning of the year. I remade it, but by that night it was short-sheeted again. It took me forever to break the spell. I had to call my father and ask him how to do it. For those of you who don't know, my father is not really the man you want to call and ask about a magical spell for a practical joke. He's a bit more serious than the rest. On the bright side, I learned a lot of new spells trying to figure it out, though I have to admit I may have misused one or two of them in the process."

Aya clapped her hands and pointed at Kathleen. "I *knew* those mirid bugs were your doing."

Izzie looked at them confused. "What type of bug?"

"They're these little bugs that look like blueberries with tiny legs. At first, they're kind of cute. They have big doe eyes, and they stare at you like they need your help. When you get close to them, though, their true nature comes out, and they roar at you as loud as a lion. The first time I came across them, they scared the living crap out of me. I've always been one to save bugs and set them free outside, but I couldn't even get near these guys."

Kathleen wrinkled her nose and shrugged. "Yeah, sorry about that. I had a feeling that's what happened. By the time I understood the spell, I couldn't find any of them. I thought maybe I'd imagined it and it somehow got fixed. Guess not."

Izzie hid a smile. She was surprised she hadn't noticed the bugs, but at the same time, she knew she hadn't noticed much of anything since her mind had been focused completely on either Luke or her dreams. The rest of the time she felt like she was walking around in a haze, but two people had helped her with that—Luke and Alison. Being around the rest of the group was an added bonus.

Luke nudged Izzie and nodded to the right, where Professor Hudson was spreading out a huge pile of long skinny sticks out on the big table. "It's s'mores time!"

Professor Hudson whistled as she twisted and flicked her wand, sending bright streams of light to different spots along what looked like a buffet. When the light petered out, the different components of s'mores appeared. There were several plates of marshmallows, more plates of chocolate bars, and graham crackers piled so high they looked as if they were going to come tumbling down on top of the students.

"Wait for it!" Emma smiled at Luke and Izzie.

Professor Hudson flicked her wand and levitated one of the marshmallows over to the fire. She held it there with her magic until it was nice and crispy.

Emma nodded. "Now *that's* the kind of magic I need to learn."

"Yeah, because magically toasting s'mores over a giant bonfire is something you're going to be facing on a regular basis." Izzie laughed.

Horace wandered up from his cottage in the teacher's quarters after changing clothes with his golden retriever by his side. He nodded at Tanner as the boy made his way over to Alison.

"Amazing fire," Tanner remarked, giving Horace two thumbs-up.

Horace chuckled. "Thanks, but the teachers get the kudos. These human hands can't do all that."

Tanner laughed and shook his head, knowing they didn't give that guy nearly enough credit

When he finally spotted Alison, he tapped her on the shoulder, grasped her hand, and kissed her on the cheek. Alison recognized the glow of his soul, The beautiful colors swirled around, still with the hint of dark still trapped by the light. She smiled and gave him a big hug.

"I was wondering where you were. I didn't see you at the banquet."

"I got here a little bit late and figured I would just come out to the bonfire," Tanner explained, squeezing her hand. "I feel like I haven't talked to you in forever."

"I know," Alison moaned. "I'm sorry about that. I couldn't talk much over the holiday because Brownstone, or my dad, I guess I should say, doesn't really understand. He thinks I should be studying, not focusing on boys, and I don't want him to give you a hard time. He's not a bad guy —I don't want you to think that. He's just kind of protective."

"Don't worry." Tanner chuckled. "I totally get it, and I really don't want to be on Brownstone's bad side."

Alison laughed. "I don't think anybody *wants* to be on his bad side, I think it just happens sometimes. But that's not the case with you. I'm trying to keep it simple, at least with him."

Tanner kissed her on the forehead and led her toward the s'mores table. "What's a bonfire without the gooey goodness of s'mores?"

"I was just thinking that myself." Alison laughed. "I was waiting for you to ask."

"You never wait on s'mores!"

Izzie smiled at the two of them and looked around to see where Luke was. She furrowed her brow when she didn't see him behind her and pushed her way through the other kids, wondering where he had gone. It really wasn't like him to just disappear, but she'd felt the tension in him. She didn't know what it was like to be a shifter with your wolf howling to get out, but she wasn't a stranger to agony.

After one loop around the courtyard, she finally found him standing in the shadows at the edge of the gardens looking toward the woods. She smiled and walked over, putting her hand on his shoulder.

"I thought I lost you."

"Nope, still right here. My hearing is exceptional as a shifter. I can hear the howling from miles away. I'm doing my best to ignore it, but sometimes it's really hard."

Izzie nodded and rubbed his arm. She reached into her pocket and pulled out a friendship bracelet. She had picked up one for him too, since he was important to her and she wanted him to know that. She held his hand palm-up and set the bracelet on it.

"I'm not sure if it'll fit you, and you don't have to wear it, but I wanted you to know just how important you are to me," Izzie whispered nervously.

Luke clutched the bracelet tightly and smiled at her. The howls of the shifters faded in his ears, his attention completely on Izzie.

"I absolutely love it, though I will have to find a chain to wear it around my neck. I don't think this will survive a shift, and I don't ever want to lose it. Thank you."

"You're welcome. Now you know that no matter what is going on, you are never alone."

"And on top of that, I get to be with the kindest and most beautiful girl in the world."

He tipped her chin up, leaned forward, and kissed her gently on the lips. She closed her eyes, feeling the sparks fly through her. His body was very warm, and he smelled like smoke and cologne. He was like a fragrant fire on a cold winter night. Warm tingles shot through her body and she leaned into him, tilting her head into his hand as he cupped her cheek. It had been her first kiss, and she couldn't imagine a more perfect one.

6

It was the first day of class since winter break. Students hurried through the hallways to the hall for breakfast or enjoyed their coffee outside in the brisk January morning. This winter had been a bit milder than the last, and the students hadn't minded a bit. They enjoyed being able to walk the grounds without having to trudge through three feet of snow.

Horace especially enjoyed it since he didn't have to shovel the teachers' walkway every morning. A little bit of salt for the ice and a quick walk-through every morning was about all Horace had to do to ensure the teachers made it up to the school safely.

Some of the students were a bit disappointed that they couldn't build snowmen like they had in the past, but that didn't stop some of them from trying. All over the grounds, tiny snowmen stood like soldiers watching the walkways. Magic energy floated around them, allowing their heads to turn as a student passed. Some even enchanted their snowmen to jump out at students who weren't paying attention, causing a bit of a ruckus at the beginning but later on laughter as some of the upperclassmen punted the snowmen into the field. It was really just fun and games, and a way to pass the time.

The library opened a second daily study hall during breakfast so that those students who had neglected to study beforehand could cram for their exams or others could finish their homework. That morning, several people took advantage of it. They'd been given a couple of reading assignments and a paper to be completed over winter break, and barely anyone had done it.

Miles, a fellow sophomore, was one of the students who had put off reading the two required chapters of the text before the first class, so he had jetted off early to Study Hall.

"Miles, you get the reading done?" one of his friends asked as he passed.

"Yeah, about ten minutes ago. I had too much going on over winter break to worry about introductory chapters for spellcasting. Isn't that what we did last year?"

His friend laughed and shook his head. "If you had actually paid attention in that class, you could say that. Considering you spent the entire semester flirting with Mabel, I would say reading the introductory chapters was probably a good idea for you."

Miles shook his head as he walked past. "Whatever. I got them read, and I'm ready for class. Besides, I aced that class last year, so paying attention apparently didn't matter."

His friend smirked. "Only because you cheated from my papers half the time. Not to mention the fact that

Mabel snuck in some of her magic to help you with spell-casting. But hey, you aced it, right?"

Miles waved his hand and kept walking as he smiled. He might have gotten off easy last year, but he knew he wouldn't have a problem. His father worked for the sector of the government that worked with magic and had taught him spells his whole life. How bad could a second-year magic class really be?

Miles tucked his hands inside the straps of his book bag and made his way toward the cafeteria. As he passed the vending machines just inside the entryway he stopped, hearing a squeaking noise. Miles turned to one of the machine and tilted his head as he slowly stepped toward it. He looked inside and narrowed his eyes at the squirrel staring back at him while happily chewing on a Payday candy bar.

Miles looked to his right and left but there was nobody else around, so he took another step forward, trying to figure out how to hell the squirrel had gotten in there. The squirrel dropped its candy bar and squealed at the top of its lungs. It pounded its little fists against the glass and rattled the entire machine. Miles jumped back and shook his head, remembering the year before and the boys' dorm squirrel incident.

"Not again!" Miles took off, leaving the squirrel behind as it retrieved the candy bar with a happy chirp.

The cafeteria was full of anxiously waiting students. They rubbed their hands together and looked down at their plates as food magically appeared. For many of them, it was their first chance to have a big breakfast since they'd left for the break. At home, where their parents were busy with work and other things, they had settled for bowls of cereal or frozen waffles.

The smell of bacon wafted throughout the cafeteria from one specific location—a table close to the stage where a third-year student sat alone. He smiled widely as he looked down at his plate, spelling more and more bacon until it was piled high.

Professor Hudson watched from the stage as the boy excitedly shoveled the bacon into his mouth. She lifted an eyebrow, walked over, and tapped the boy on his shoulder. The boy cringed and slowly looked up at the teacher as she scowled down at him. She crossed her arms and lifted both eyebrows, nodding at his overflowing plate of bacon.

"Part of having a good day is starting with a nutritious breakfast. Well-rounded should be the word of the day for you, which means I expect you to add a little fruit to that plate of pork."

"Yes, ma'am." The boy sighed, and she nodded as she walked back to her seat.

He let out a deep breath of defeat and looked down at his plate of bacon.

"Stupid fruit," he muttered under his breath.

Slowly a smile emerged on his face. He nodded at the plate, and a single strawberry appeared on top of the bacon. He glanced at Eleanor, who just shook her head and went back to drinking her coffee as his friends joined him. They laughed and poked fun at him but followed right along, piling their plates with bacon, sausage, and a single piece of fruit.

Leo looked up from his plate at Professor Hudson as she chuckled. She shrugged and set her coffee cup down.

"I guess you can't win them all." She sighed.

"One day those kids will look back and wish they had listened to you. Of course, it won't be until their doctor tells them their arteries are made of bacon." Leo laughed loudly.

Professor Hudson chuckled again, picked up the one piece of turkey bacon on her plate, and saluted the boys with it. She figured if she couldn't beat them, she might as well join them.

"Why does half the male population in this cafeteria look like they're ready to get up and run at a moment's notice?" Kathleen asked, popping a piece of watermelon into her mouth.

"Because today is the day they tell us officially if we made the Louper team," Luke explained with excitement.

Ethan gave him a high five and shoveled a spoonful of Captain Crunch into his mouth. "You already know you made it, Luke. It's not like Coach would have lied to you."

Izzie was nervous for Luke. She knew it meant a lot to him, so she faced the door of the cafeteria, waiting for him to return.

"Don't worry," Alison whispered, seeing the streams of anxiety in Izzie's energy.

"Ugh," she groaned rolling her eyes. "I just want things

to go right for him, you know? He has already endured so much, being a shifter and all, and if something changed, it would kill his spirits."

"What about your spirits?"

Izzie squeezed Alison's hand. "I'll worry about that when the time comes."

After about five minutes and a whole bunch of cheers from outside, Luke walked back through the door with a huge smile on his face, followed by Ethan with a slightly confused look on his.

"I did make the team," Luke confirmed proudly. He leaned down and kissed Izzie on the cheek. "And surprisingly, even though he just helped and practiced a bit out of curiosity, the coach put Ethan on the team as well."

"Wow! That's really exciting!"

"Thanks. Of course, that's just the first step. I have to work my butt off and do the best that I can, on and off the field. Everything I walk into that game with is transferred to my character, so I have to be prepared."

"I'm sure you will kill it out there. Besides, you are amazing, so your character should be on the up and up."

Luke smiled at her and squeezed her shoulder. "Speaking of being on the up and up, they put up the results for the play you tried out for. You should go check it out."

"Yes!" Kathleen squealed, nearly choking on her fruit. "Come on, woman, get up! We have to see where you will be debuting your Hollywood talent!"

Alison stood up and pulled Izzie from her chair. Izzie still had nerves running through her energy. "Deep breaths. You either got the part, or you didn't. Either way, you did phenomenally, or so everyone except Scarlett has been saying."

"Right," Izzie replied, letting out a deep breath and walking with Alison and Kathleen to the list. "Deep breaths. Not the end of the world."

There was a crowd around the list, and at least five freshmen rolling their eyes.

"Great, a freaking flying monkey. My mother will be so proud," he groaned to his friend.

It didn't take Izzie long to find her name right at the top, listed next to Dorothy. She let out a whoop and covered her mouth. It was just the morale boost she needed. She'd figured after she'd knocked almost everyone down with a burst of energy that she probably hadn't gotten the part, but it looked like that wasn't the case.

"I got it! I actually got the part of Dorothy!" Izzie laughed, squeezing Alison's hand hard.

"I knew you could do it. It's not a surprise to me at all."

"This is so exciting," Kathleen sang out, gripping her other hand. "You were pretty much made for that part."

"God, I hope so," Izzie replied with a laugh. "Because I'm going to be playing it in front of the entire school."

"Don't get nervous now," Alison replied. "You haven't even started rehearsal."

"Exactly, and trust me—once you are comfortable with your lines and the other actors, you will lose those nerves in like two seconds," Kathleen told her.

"Really? I—" She paused when a low whisper moved through the crowd.

Scarlett stomped through, pushing Alison and Izzie to the sides, and put her hands on her hips—and her smug face dropped. Two spots down, Scarlett was listed as the Good Witch, something she did not look pleased about in the least.

She huffed and smacked her hands down by her sides, turning quickly toward Izzie. She shook her finger in her face.

"I guess the part is perfect for you. An orphan playing an orphan." With that, Scarlet stormed off through her group of minions, huffing and puffing all the way.

Alison smirked turning toward Izzie's excited energy and shrugged her shoulders. "Not happy about not being Dorothy, I guess?" Izzie laughed and took Alison's hand.

The two of them spotted Kathleen by the staircase with an armload of posters. They hadn't even seen her walk away. They certainly had no idea how she'd had time to grab that many posters, but one thing they knew about Kathleen was that she was undercover-sneaky and knew more magic than she let on.

She waved her wand and several of the posters flew through the air and stuck themselves to the walls. She smiled at Alison and Izzie and handed Izzie one of the posters.

"I'm running for class president for next year," Kathleen said excitedly. "My father helped me make the posters. I realized this morning that voting was coming up soon, so I figured I might as well get them out now."

Izzie looked down at the poster and smiled. To the right in big bold letters, the poster read, Kathleen for Junior Class President! Below the heading and to the left were magically-boosted photos of Kathleen both in Paris and the islands during her summer and winter breaks. They moved like videos on the paper: Kathleen running, laughing, and looking fabulous, just like she always did. At the bottom was another magically-boosted photo where she blew a kiss to the viewer of the poster and sent little magical hearts floating out like bubbles. It was exactly what you would expect from Kathleen, and surprisingly Izzie loved it.

7

U p and down the halls, students perused the dozens of posters that represented different grade levels, positions, and candidates running for office for the next school year. Each was exciting and highlighted a specific characteristic of the student it had been created for. Some students showed their athletic ability, putting up stats from their chosen sport and posing for pictures that ensured their muscles were on display.

"Vote Brock. I have the strength of a king," a poster called as a group of girls walked past.

"You don't have to twist my arm." The girls giggled.

Other candidates showed their academic prowess, and still others, like Kathleen, showed the excitement of their lives outside of school.

"Vote Naomi. I've been around the world, this one and Oriceran. I can tell you now that if anyone knows how to solve a problem, it's me!"

"Vote Alfie. I'm not only Earth-born, but I have strong

connections on Oriceran—the perfect magical mixture this school needs!"

Several of the posters were accompanied by music or a short speech to draw the students in with promises, and political quotes the candidates hoped would get the student body pumped. Regardless of what the poster said or showed they were all magically-enhanced, making the elections a lot more exciting than a normal high school's.

Kathleen was running for class president for their junior year, while Wyatt was running for student body president against Scarlett. Both Wyatt and Scarlett were popular choices for student body president, although they appealed to two very different groups of people.

"I like Wyatt," one of the girls said. "He is smart, handsome, rich, and is like the nicest person in our school. I feel like he genuinely cares."

"Yeah, but...Scarlett is incredibly gifted in magic, and we all know that's an excellent thing when it comes to leading and getting things done. Besides, I'm not taking the chance of getting caught voting against her. She can be terrifying."

"Great, now we are voting based on fear. I'm going to start calling her 'Stalin.'"

It was true. Most people were actually terrified of her, but this was both a good thing and a bad thing for her. Some people felt obligated to vote for her, fearful of the retribution they might receive if they didn't, while others hoped for a better future and were immediately drawn to Wyatt.

"Look," Scarlett began, turning to the others following her around, "I know people are scared of me. I know that some are jumping ship to swim toward the island of Wyatt for safekeeping, but we can't let that ruin the chance of me winning. I have to be nice and so do you guys, so as of right now, no freshmen pranks until further notice."

As Scarlett walked down the hallway toward the class-rooms, she plastered on a fake smile and waved at the different students along the way. She was trying to be on her best behavior. She couldn't quite pull it off when it came to Izzie and the part of Dorothy, but to the rest of the school, she was a shining example—helpful, kind, and trustworthy.

Of course, Izzie's group and many of the other students knew better, but her focus was solely on the younger kids. They wanted to fit in—and desperately wanted to stay out of her way.

"I need you to make sure that there are no other posters anywhere near mine," Scarlett whispered to one of her cronies. "Especially Wyatt's. His poster sends out a magical fog that covers the other posters around his, so the students focus only on him. It's a cheap trick, but not against the rules."

One of her groupies looked at her and raised an eyebrow. "Since when do you play by the rules? Why don't you just do the same, or do something to his posters?"

Scarlett pressed her fingers to her lips. "Because, idiot, if I want to get elected, I have to show that I play fair—or at least play fair during the elections. I have to look better than Wyatt, and we all know how many people just love him. It's gross, and I don't get it, but it is what it is. So until I'm elected, which I will be, we'll play by the rules."

Scarlett plastered on another smile. She walked over to

one of the freshmen and turned her back to the teacher down the hall. The freshman was desperately filling in the answers to a homework assignment she'd forgotten to do, and she looked at Scarlett with a bit of fear in her eyes. Scarlett smiled and put her hand on the girl's.

"Here, let me help you with that," she offered sweetly, waving her hand over the paper. The answers appeared in the student's handwriting.

The student goggled at the paper and thanked Scarlett.

"No problem." Scarlett forced a smile. "Make sure you let your friends know. Vote for me for Student Body President!"

"For sure," the student called as she rushed to class.

Scarlett turned to her groupies and put out her hands. "See, that's exactly what we need to be doing, and don't forget to tell them to vote for me for student body president. It's important—no, *vital*—that she says my name and exactly what position I'm running for. Otherwise, they might just assume it's Wyatt, the nicest guy on earth, helping them out. I need everyone to nod if they understand."

This wasn't the first time Scarlett had done something for one of the younger kids. She'd done small magical deeds behind the teachers' backs for weeks in an attempt to win the favor of the majority. She also had her friends, or her minions, as Kathleen called them, follow her everywhere and do the same with as many students as she possibly could find. It seemed to be working, and Wyatt was frustrated by the number of underclassmen supporting Scarlett.

Standing in the shadows to the left and holding a pile of

flyers was the third, less-known student body president candidate, Farrell.

"Who is that?" Claire asked Scarlett.

Scarlett looked over with a fake smile that quickly faded. "The other guy running. He's a shifter or something, and apparently, he is just doing it to raise awareness. No one actually thinks he will be elected. He's shy and quiet, and of course, there's the whole wolf thing."

One of Scarlett's minions walked up and glanced in the direction of Scarlett's stare. "I heard he's a fourth-generation shifter from Maine and has been having a hard time controlling his dog, so his parents sent him here."

Shifters had always kept to themselves or with their packs and didn't really socialize with the others in the magical community. Up until twenty years before, the fear of shifters hadn't even come close to what it was now. During one of the many rises of the dark families on Earth, one specific dark family had decided that they would attempt an experiment, creating new shifters from kidnapped humans. At first, it seemed like the idea was perfect. The dark family thought they'd created a race of wild beasts that was theirs to command, one that would attack the light magic beings and anyone in their way. However, it didn't take long for the dark family to realize that this plan was seriously flawed.

The shifters didn't listen to just anyone. They only listened to their pack leader, the Alpha. Since their creation, the shifters had turned their backs on the dark family, taken out some of the main members, and tried to reclaim their lives.

Anyone who knew the dark families was sure they'd

retaliate, and during a very delicate time between humans and the magical community, the dark families started their revenge. They poisoned the shifters in public settings, including places of work within the human community, rallies in the middle of big cities, and during commute hours when it was crucial that a shifter control their powers. The magical community was aware of the issue, but bad blood had already spread, and it stayed that way for many years.

"Farrell for Student Body President," he called as he handed a group one of his flyers.

He'd asked one of the professors to help him create a magical poster, but it wasn't anything like the others. He just didn't possess the skills that they did, and he was okay with that. His platform was based on the premise that he would be an excellent link between the magicals and the non-magicals. To help the two groups learn how to interconnect without outing themselves. The teachers thought it was a fantastic idea, but the kids thought it was lackluster and boring.

One of the boys took the flyer and scoffed, then balled it up and tossed it over his shoulder. "If I wanted a dog to represent me, I'd bring my German Shepherd in. At least he knows how to behave in public."

Farrell didn't say a word, just sighed and leaned down to pick up the wadded-up flyer. He tossed it in the recycling bin. He was used to that response. He knew it was very unlikely that he'd win, but he figured it was about time the shifters tried harder to become part of the regular scenery in the magical community.

"Hey, dude." Allen, one of his friends and fellow shifters,

smiled, walking up and patting him on the back. "You bringing the masses into your cause?"

Farrell scoffed. "Hardly. More like standing here as an easy target between classes."

"Hey, man, don't let it get you down. You knew this would be tough, but it's definitely a move in the right direction."

Around the corner, a group of dark witches and wizards emerged, laughing and talking amongst themselves. Farrell gripped his flyers tighter, and his eyes flashed amber. Allen squared up beside him and looked at them, trying not to catch their attention.

"I hate that so many of the dark families' kids are allowed here," Farrell grumbled. "It's a good way to ensure really bad things go down."

"Yeah, I get it, and so do the rest of the shifters. Some of the seniors even transferred out before this year. Their families didn't want them to have to deal with the dark kids—not that I can blame them. A lot of their parents were either victims twenty years ago, or they remembered the event all too well."

The dark witches and wizards spotted Farrell and Allen and elbowed each other. The leader of the group nodded at his friends and tried to cover a smirk as he walked over to the shifters.

"You mind if I get a flyer?"

Farrell just stared at him, but Allen cleared his throat and puffed out his chest. "I thought you dark kids didn't care about this stuff?"

The dark magic kid gritted his teeth and shifted his

stare to Farrell. "We don't. We were just curious how our creations were doing out here in the world."

Farrell stepped into the wizard's face. "Say that again, but this time picture your creation ripping your throat out."

"Farrell, don't let him get to you. He's just mad that his parents sent him here instead of training him themselves. It must suck to be one of the rejects."

The wizard's wand dropped from inside his sleeve to his hand as Headmistress Berens rounded the corner. She glanced right past them at first, but then stopped, walked over, and eyed the three of them. The others moved away at her approach. She cleared her throat and held her wand in her hand, unsure what was going on.

"You boys should be in class. You're not having an issue, are you?"

The dark wizard smirked and took a flyer out of Farrell's hand. "No, Headmistress. No problem at all. Just seeing what this candidate has to offer. It may not be enough to pique my interest, though."

The headmistress looked at the wizard with narrowed eyes, then looked at Farrell, who seemed to be struggling to keep it together. "Go to class, and I don't want to see you or your group out here again. Do you understand that?"

The dark kids nodded and disappeared around the corner, scoffing and grumbling about the headmistress. She let out a sigh and looked at Farrell, who was still clutching his flyers. She glanced at Allen and gave him a nod.

"Why don't you boys get some air to clear your minds? We don't need any accidents this year."

8

E leanor Hudson stood at the front of the class, going through papers on her desk while waiting for everyone to get settled. The students slowly trickled in, with the second bell only moments from ringing. The desks were arranged in pairs, and Alison and Izzie sat together. They assumed they'd be paired off for whatever lessons were scheduled in second-year spells class that day.

Just as the second bell rang Ethan ran in and took a seat next to Peter, ignoring Professor Hudson's glare over the top of her glasses. She flicked her wand at the back door and it slowly shut. One last student squeezed through before it latched.

She cleared her throat and put her hands on the lectern. "Welcome back to school. I hope you had an excellent holiday season. I also hope that each and every one of you read the chapters you were assigned before coming back. If you did not, you might just have a little bit of a problem with our next lesson. Now, in today's class, we are going to learn to regulate a spell that will allow you to create something and then undo it slowly and carefully. Please pair off. You will be working with the piece of wood on your desk."

All the students looked at their empty desks and wondered what she was talking about. Without glancing their way, she flicked her wand. A steady stream of white light moved through the classroom, bounced off each desk, and deposited a large chunk of wood in front of each student. A quiet whisper moved across the classroom. Even in their second-year, students never got tired of watching things appear and disappear with the flick of their professors' wands.

"The spell to change a piece of wood into glass is 'Splinter fragile changus.' Then, simply reverse the spell by saying, 'Changus fragile splinter.' I would like everybody to take a moment and try it. Remember to focus on a slow and steady change."

All the students either pulled out their wands or readied themselves to create the spell, then a collective whisper of the enchantment flowed through the classroom. Small flashes of light flickered over the desks as the wood changed into glass. Izzie looked at Alison and smiled as she stared at the energy in front of her. It shifted from the shape of a large piece of wood to the shape of a goblet. Alison verified with a touch that it was glass.

"Very good." Professor Hudson clapped. "Now, I want everyone to reverse it, but remember to do it slowly."

Izzie held her hands out with her palms forward and pulled just a bit of energy from her chest. The white light swirled around her glass and slowly changed it back to a chunk of wood. Since no one in the class seemed to have any issues with this type of spell, Professor Hudson saw no reason to linger on it. She swished her wand, and the wood was replaced with a dish of water.

"Excellent! Let's move on to something just a bit harder. You're going to lift the water from the bowl, separate it into droplets, levitate them for ten to fifteen seconds, then put the drops back into the bowl without a splash. The spell for this is, 'Levitates droplets,' and then, 'Return to form.'"

Each student took their time creating the spell, and watched the droplets separate and swirl above the bowl. Alison sensed the energy lifting from the bowl of water into the air and saw it separate into sparkling orbs of light. She smiled as she danced her fingers back and forth and the drops twisted and turned, changing colors. She whispered the reversal spell and giggled as the droplets slowly fell back into the bowl.

Izzie looked at her and smiled. The spell wasn't hard, but it was fun to do. She really enjoyed working on magic with her best friend.

Ethan, however, was less amused. "When will I ever need to know this?"

Professor Hudson removed her glasses and whipped her wand toward Ethan. She shot a long stream of white light toward him, which wrapped around his legs and up to his stomach. Ethan dropped his wand, put his hands in the air, and stood, knocking over his chair. The entire class stared as Professor Hudson quickly lifted Ethan to the ceiling and flicked her wand, letting him drop back toward the floor. There was a collective gasp across the classroom as they watched her catch Ethan at the last moment with a swirl of her wand.

"Creeping Movement," she whispered, using the spell to slow him down. She laid him carefully on the floor.

Ethan rolled onto his back and stared at the ceiling, and Professor Hudson walked over and looked down at him. He nodded silently. She'd just demonstrated exactly how the spell could be used. Giggles and murmurs flew through the classroom as Peter reached down to help Ethan to his feet. His cheeks were red with embarrassment, and he shook his head and sat back down at his desk to continue the spell. Kathleen looked at them and smirked. It wasn't often she saw Ethan embarrassed by anything, but she decided not to give him a hard time—at least not yet. She would save that ammo for another day.

Eleanor returned to the front of the class, put her glasses back on, sat down behind her desk, and observed the students as they quickly went back to work. A couple of the students struggled with the spell. The water from their bowls spilled out over the desk and down onto the floor. Professor Hudson used her magic to mop up the mess and refilled their bowls, then showed them exactly what they were doing wrong. When the last of the students had successfully completed the task, she swished her wand and the bowls disappeared. She glanced up at the clock and realized they still had over half of the class left. She flipped open her book and ran her finger down to the next lesson.

"Since everyone seems to have a very good grasp on these lessons, we're going to go ahead and move on to a more difficult spell. This lesson isn't actually supposed to start until next week, but I think this would be a good chance to give it some practice before testing begins. We're going to be creating objects out of shadows."

A whisper of excitement blew over the class, and Eleanor put her hand up to quiet them down. "I'm not going to assign a specific item that I'd like you to create. I want you all to use your imagination, remembering that it must be an *object*, not a living thing, and of course appropriate for the classroom. The enchantment for this specific spell is, '*Shadow contortus.*'"

The students went to work immediately, excited to try this spell. Kathleen and Emma started out by turning the shadow beneath their desk into a teacup. The teacup quietly rattled on the floor before turning back into a shadow. Eleanor clapped her hands and nodded at Kathleen and Emma for a job well done. Izzie looked at the window, held her hands out, closed her eyes, and felt the energy build in her chest. Symbols slowly flipped over on her arms and neck, and her skin glowed brightly. She released the energy from her palm while whispering the enchantment under her breath.

When she opened her eyes, she found that the shadow had twisted and turned into a vine that moved across the wall and over the edge of the open window. She closed her hands and centered her energy, pulling back as the vine shifted and turned back into a shadow. Eleanor nodded at Izzie and smiled, then watched Alison as she prepared to do the spell. Alison was excited, and though she couldn't see exactly what the shadow turned into, she could see the glow of magic around her. As she began to pull the energy in through her chest and down her arms, feeling the tingle at her fingertips, she heard the whispers from the girls behind her.

"Did you know that Tanner and Izzie are not only a couple, but they're both orphans? Maybe we have not just one, but two toombies among us."

Alison gritted her teeth and closed her eyes against the surge of anger that blew through her. Instantly and without her knowledge, the shadow by the window morphed into a sword. Its edge gleamed from the stream of light coming through. Without a sound and without Alison even muttering the words to the spell, the sword neatly cut through the blinds, then hovered in the air next to the windowsill. The entire class fell silent, staring at the still-present sword and watching the edges of the broken blinds flap in the breeze. Alison noted the silence and realized just how much anger she had built up inside.

Izzie's eyes grew large, and she touched her friend's arm with a gasp. "Alison..."

Instantly, Alison let the anger go and opened her eyes. She saw the magic around the windowsill. It ran up and down through the shades and flowed out into the courtyard beyond the classroom. She had no idea what had happened, but from the red streaks through the magic's energy, she knew it had been done in anger. Izzie whipped her narrow-eyed gaze to the two girls behind them with a scowl. The girls shrugged and looked down abashedly at the papers in front of them. They hadn't realized that Izzie was in front of them when they'd started gossiping about something they knew nothing about.

Eleanor's eyes were wide, but she quickly collected herself and took a deep breath. She did not want the other students to know that what had just happened was beyond most of the students' ability. "Well done, Alison. Nicely done."

Eleanor swished her wand and calmly whispered a spell to restore the blind. Her professor's calm tone relaxed Alison, and the sword shook quietly by the windowsill before turning back into a shadow and drifting out the open window. She sat down in her chair and dropped her hands in her lap, knowing she had just done something that she hadn't had any control over. Her Drow powers were growing. This wasn't the first time she'd unconsciously done something with her magic.

Izzie looked around the classroom and realized that the students weren't as freaked out as she'd thought they would be. Instead, they seemed even more excited to do the spell. They all started trying to make their own weapons, and it wasn't long before the professor caught on. She lifted her hand and frowned, speaking sternly to the class.

"No weapons!"

Alison refrained from trying the spell again for the rest of the class. Eleanor was aware that Alison was struggling with what had just happened, but there wasn't much she could say to make the girl feel better. It was obvious that her powers were stronger than she realized. Unfortunately, Professor Hudson had little knowledge of Drow magic and feared that any attempt to help would only make things worse. Although this hadn't been the first time Alison had faced something difficult, when it came to her magic, the Drow girl was alone. Eleanor wished that her mother or someone who knew about Drow magic was there to help and guide her. If Alison didn't get control, it was only a matter of time before she would hurt someone, or even worse, do it without meaning to. That was the last thing she wanted to happen. She knew what magic was capable of. She'd seen it with her own eyes, and she had felt the loss in her own heart.

9

For the rest of the day, Alison contemplated exactly what had happened in the spells class. Suffice it to say, she wasn't extremely excited when they walked into Professor Powell's class and found out that the lesson for the day was how to break through glamours. She'd hoped that they would go the rest of the day without her having to use magic, but she was in a school for magic so she couldn't be upset about it. She took her seat next to Izzie and waited for class to begin. Izzie grasped her hand and squeezed it to comfort her. Alison smiled and squeezed back, thankful for her best friend.

"All right, class, let's just jump straight into today's lesson. We're going to be breaking through Glamours, or at least learning how to do so. To accomplish this, we have to go over a few things."

Professor Powell turned his back to the class and began writing on the chalkboard with his wand. Seated in the row in front with Izzie and Alison were several of the dark children, clustered together, joking around and not paying attention. Winter, one of the dark kids, had always seemed relatively nice compared to the others. He always stood at the back, never really laughed at the pranks the wizards pulled, and when no one else was around, he was really nice to Alison and Izzie. However, it was obvious that he was trying to fit in with the other kids that day. The wizard next to him nudged him and glanced at Alison.

"I wonder if she can make it through class this time without kung fu-chopping something in half with a magical shadow?"

Both of them laughed. Winter just rolled his eyes at Alison and Izzie. Izzie gritted her teeth and rested her hands palms up beneath the desk and let the energy flow down her arms to collect in her palms. She flicked the fingers of her right hand and pelted both Winter and the other kid in the back of the head with pea-sized fireballs. Winter's yelp brought Xander Powell's sharp gaze back to the class. Izzie shifted uncomfortably in her seat, but Winter kept his silence, even as his friends shot threats at Izzie.

"It looks like we might need to teach the orphan a lesson." They chuckled.

Alison squeezed Izzie's hand and leaned toward her. "Let it go. Totally not worth it."

From Izzie's other side Ethan leaned in, muttering, "Who names their kid after a season?"

Xander finished the last dot of the I, and with a nervous face reminded the class just how important it was to understand the threat of dark magic. "I know I've said this a hundred times, but I'll continue to repeat it until I'm sure all of you understand. The point of learning the history of dark magic and how it works is so that you can learn how to counter it, not so you can use it. Now, I would like three volunteers to come up to the front of the class and give themselves a glamour."

Xander raised an eyebrow as he waited for someone to volunteer. After a few moments and the fear that he would randomly pick people, two Light Elves and a wizard raised their hands. Xander nodded and waved them up to the front of the class.

"Go ahead and put on your glamour, then concentrate on maintaining it. I'm going to try to break it with a spell, but don't be scared. I have full control of my magic."

The three volunteers quickly put on a glamour. Two of them made themselves look more human and less elf, and the wizard turned himself into a large furry creature. Xander chuckled and nodded, then pulled out his wand and whispered the incantation under his breath." *Crackus Fakeness.*" With a swish of his wand, sparkling strands of white magic whipped between the three volunteers, then shot toward the ceiling and showered them with sparkles. The two elves quickly lost their glamour. Their ears turned pointy once again, and their skins lost the dark tan they had given themselves. The wizard's glamour, on the other hand, didn't crack, and Xander laughed at the challenge. He shot an even stronger bolt of magic, and the wizard flickered between his real self and his glamoured furry creature until finally the boy stood there.

One after another the kids in the class challenged the professor with their glamours. Of course, Professor Powell was proficient with his magic and was able to shoot them down one at a time. After about twenty minutes Izzie stood up, excited, but as Xander looked at her, she hesitated. She thought he was going to tell her to sit down, and in truth, he was. After a moment, though, he decided to try a different spell on her.

Purple and green sparks shot from the end of Xander's wand, and without thought, Izzie immediately raised her hands. Energy coursed through her as she created a shield that wrapped around her body. It was almost as if she had recognized the spell before it'd been cast, and her reaction surprised her. Professor Powell's spell bounced off the radiating waves of sound she'd created, but the resulting sweet chime everyone else heard was lost to Izzie as a thought blew through her mind.

This was the first piece of magic my mother ever taught me.

Izzie's head shot up, and she dropped the shields. Professor Powell lowered his wand at the same time. He wasn't prepared for the look of shock that crossed her face. Her eyes glistened as tears built up. She was startled by her thought and by her ability to do magic she had no memory of learning, and amazed that she might have just remembered something about her mother. It felt like time stood still as the thought repeated in her mind. Alison observed the streams of stress and sadness curling through her energy and saw the spell dissipate. She didn't know what had happened, but from the looks of it, Izzie had had some sort of realization.

Izzie didn't know if it had been a realization, but she *did* know that there was something inside trying to tell her about her mother. It was like a blast of energy hit her straight in the chest, and she didn't know which way to turn. That thought, combined with her dreams and her nightmares, started to make those things all too real for her. She was tired of not understanding or knowing, and having so many unanswered questions. Izzie tried to figure out where that thought had come from, She searched for more, and tried to remember when she'd first learned magic before it slipped away.

My mother? I knew her? She's alive?

A tear slid down Izzie's cheek, and she felt the wetness. Suddenly, she remembered that she was in class, surrounded by classmates. Without looking around, she grabbed her books and ran out of the room.

Kathleen, Aya, Emma, and Alison were already out of their chairs and headed for the door to chase after Izzie. The professor knew, though, that Izzie needed some time to herself. Some time to figure out what was going on and calm herself enough to sort through her mind. He swished his wand and created a barrier in front of the door. The girls bounced off it and slid across the floor on their butts. They looked over their shoulders at the professor, who raised an eyebrow at them and gestured to their seats before turning back toward the board.

"Where were we?"

Once the girls were seated, the professor paused for just a moment and concern crossed his face. He wondered if they knew he was suspicious about Izzie. He had always wondered about the girl, and as her magic grew, so did his suspicions. He cleared his throat and continued teaching the class, knowing there was nothing he could do about it at that point. He would definitely keep his eye on her, though. Mara kept Izzie close, and not just because she was an orphan. He knew the headmistress better than that, and he suspected there was something more to Izzie than what they'd been told—or even what *she'd* been told. She was extraordinarily powerful, and her powers grew by leaps and bounds with each day that passed. Even for a growing young elf, this wasn't the norm.

Xander wasn't the only one, either. Izzie had her own suspicions about many different things—not just her powers, but her past as well. As she ran through the halls with tears streaming down her face, she thought about all the strange memories and dreams she'd had recently. She thought about how strong her powers were. How it didn't make any sense when they had said she was a Light Elf, and how strict Mara Berens had been since she'd arrived at the School of Necessary Magic.

Izzie hit the top of the steps, ran through the empty dorms into her room, threw open the door, and shut it quickly behind her. She leaned against the door for a moment, sobbing uncontrollably into her hands. She felt like she couldn't breathe or think. It was like something inside her was trying to break free and tell her exactly who she was. At the same time, though, something very strong blocked those memories. It was almost like Izzie had a foreign power inside her.

She walked to her bed and dropped her books on it, then lowered herself to the floor in front of the footboard. She covered her mouth to muffle her sobs. She knew her friends would try to follow her, but she hoped none of them could find her, at least for the moment. She was too upset, and she didn't want to have to explain everything to all of them. Alison was the only one she had told about her dreams, her thoughts, and her powers which increased by the day, and she had only done that yesterday. Even with that, Alison didn't know everything. Izzie just wanted a moment to figure it out in her head.

She took a deep breath and leaned her head back against the footboard, blinking the tears from her eyes, and stared at the light on the ceiling. She tried to let the emotions drain from her, giving herself a moment to think about what had happened. She ran her hands through her hair and gripped the back of her head while drawing her knees to her chest. She'd thought that maybe if she had a moment alone she could start to understand what she was missing, but instead, the time between when she left the classroom and when she got to the dorm had been long enough to release the memory from her mind. Frustrated, she slammed her hands against the floor and shook her head.

"Why can't I remember?"

I zzie dramatically read her line. "Oh, Toto, I've a feeling we're not in Kansas anymore."

It was another rehearsal of *the Wizard of Oz*, something they'd done almost every day this week. The performance date was drawing closer, and although Izzie had picked up all her lines without a problem, several of the others were struggling. As they rehearsed the characters moved on and off the stage, practicing stage right and stage left, trying to remember to face the audience, and dealing with the light crew accidentally shining spotlights into their faces.

Scarlett, who really hated playing the Good Witch, tried to make the best of her time whenever her character was not needed. She stood off to the side and practiced being nice to different people without rolling her eyes. She figured if she was going to be a good actress, that was the best place to start. How hard could it be, after all? She'd acted in a dozen plays, and this was only an extension of that. She just had to walk the halls, pretend she actually liked people, and attempt to help them without showing how nauseated it made her, regardless of whether she liked it. She knew that to win the election, she needed to give the performance of a lifetime.

Back onstage, Izzie went through her lines with Winter. He'd been cast as the Tin Man and was doing a pretty good job at it. Half the time, he was friendly to Izzie. He'd hold conversations, help her with her lines, and act like any other student in the school. The other half—when his friends were watching—he'd look at them and snicker as if they had some grand plan to screw Izzie over. She didn't know which Winter to believe, so she just ignored it. She enjoyed it when he was kind, and focused on the play whenever he was laughing with his friends. She didn't have the time or patience to deal with someone who couldn't just be themselves. Izzie wished that Winter was pleasant all the time. She knew it was in him, but there was too much going on in her life to try to help him with his. She just hoped the two of them could get through the play cordially, without his friends causing too much trouble.

Luke stopped by the auditorium for a few minutes to watch Izzie practice without her knowledge. He started down the aisle but stopped in his tracks when he saw Winter next to Izzie on the stage. Luke was very aware of who Winter was, along with all his dark friends who had gone out of their way to give him a hard time because he was a shifter. He hadn't, however, known that Winter was in the play with Izzie. For some reason, he didn't like Winter being anywhere near her, even if he was being nice to her at the moment. His eyes flashed Amber and he narrowed them, letting out a low growl before walking out of the auditorium.

He wanted to stay and watch over Izzie since there were so many members of the dark families present, but he knew she could take care of herself, and he had Louper practice to get to. He was already late because he'd been stuck in study hall after being caught laughing with one of his friends. He shuffled down the hallway past some of the classrooms and went through the door to the gym. Inside was a group of freshmen playing the magical version of dodgeball. He stopped for just a moment, knowing there was no way he could miss that.

The large red ball chased the students and picked them off one by one with no mercy. A larger freshman, round in the middle, stood staring up at the bleachers, completely oblivious to everything around him. As if the ball could sense his lack of focus on the game, it soared through the air and hit the oversized boy right in the butt, sending him to the floor on all fours. Luke covered his mouth to hide the laugh that vibrated in his chest. The big red ball ricocheted off the boy and slammed into one of the freshman girls' heads, knocking her on her side and sending her sliding across the floor. One of the freshman boys to his right looked much more enthusiastic about the game than he should. The kid was bent at the knees with his hands out in front, obviously ready to have a go at the ball.

"I got this!" the kid yelled, putting one hand in the air. His eyes stayed glued to the ball.

Luke lifted an eyebrow, ready for the kid to be completely wiped out. They were clearly trying to beat Izzie's record from the semester before, but she was still the champion for holding on the longest during a game of dodgeball. As the ball whizzed through the air, the boy made a valiant effort. He jumped and grabbed it, clenching his fingers tightly and holding on for dear life. At first, his face was focused, but as the ball began to buck, shooting straight up in the air and back down and jerking side to side, he quickly lost his concentration.

Luke chuckled loudly as the ball faked right and launched the kid into the other students nearby. They rolled across the floor and laid there as the ball slammed into the last two students standing, then did a victory lap around the top of the gym wall. Luke had been impressed by the attempt, but he was even more entertained by the domino effect of the kids falling over when the would-be champion slammed into them. From the looks of it, they had been playing the game for quite a while. Almost everyone looked sweaty, tired, and ready to call it quits. However, a few of the freshman still had that look of determination. Luke knew they wouldn't quit until someone had won the game, even if they didn't break the record this time.

Luke smiled and kept walking, wishing he had a few more minutes to watch the chaos. Louper practice was much more important, though. As he passed the classrooms where the Entrepreneur Club met, he heard Grace, Peter, and Ethan talking back and forth. It was a big day for Grace—she was unveiling her blueprints and the prototype Peter had made for her to the rest of the group. They hadn't had much time to work on it, but Peter thought it would be better if she showed the technology to everyone instead of just a sketch. So, they had gotten together each evening, sometimes with Ethan, to work on the prototype and work out some of the issues before it was time to make the presentation.

"I would love to stay and watch all this happen," Ethan said triumphantly. "Unfortunately, for you, I have Louper practice, so I gotta get out of here. Let me know how it goes."

Ethan ran from the classroom, nodding at Luke as he passed and jogged down the hallway. He'd left all his gear in his dorm, so he had to go there first to get it. Luke was just happy he wasn't the only one who was going to be late to practice, even if it was Ethan, who was late for everything. Grace noticed Luke standing outside the classroom and smiled and waved just before Peter walked in front of her. Peter held the prototype up proudly and began to explain the internal workings of Grace's proposal to fix the issues they'd had last year. Peter really thought he had done well this time, carefully putting it together and pushing the amount of magic into it that it needed.

"We worked hard on this prototype. It may have some issues we haven't sorted out yet, but we are hoping it will give you a really good idea of how hard Grace worked on this over winter break to help get this project off the ground," Peter explained, trying to sound confident.

Peter looked at Grace, who nodded excitedly and turned on her phone. Peter took a deep breath, opened the prototype's front cover, and pressed the green button. For a brief moment, as the lights flashed on the screen, he thought he had actually done it. He thought he had actually put together the prototype in such a way that it wouldn't explode in his face. But he knew it was unlikely.

Luke grimaced as a flash of light brightened the classroom, accompanied by a loud bang that shook the pictures on the wall. Dense smoke billowed out of the classroom and down the hall, indicating to Luke that it was probably time to move on. He shook his head and walked away fast to escape the rancid smell.

He turned into another hall, but if he were looking for quiet, that was not the place to find it. As he moved through the corridor, the posters for every single political race spoke to him. He glanced from side to side, feeling kind of awkward. He wasn't used to that much magic in one place. All the candidates' eyes followed him as he walked. It looked almost as if each person were trapped in the poster taped or pinned to the walls. They all spoke at once, explaining why they were the best choice for the office and exhorting him to remember their face.

Luke took a deep breath and shook his head. "How am I supposed to remember your faces when there are so many of you? And how in the hell am I supposed to know what you're saying with all of your voices producing a magical harmony of political bullcrap?"

He laughed as he turned the corner into the foyer. The voices had stopped, and he paused for a moment to enjoy the silence. There was nothing on the boards except for the magical ROTC sign-up sheet, which was completely void of signatures. There wasn't a single soul in the school who trusted the government enough to join the military program run by humans, even though they attended a government-funded school. Even the shifters, many of them sharing their heritage with humans, knew there were too many risks and too many reasons the government might turn against them in the future.

No matter how fiercely Mara Berens attempted to get someone to sign up for the program, there had been no takers. She had even tried bribing some of the students with free passes to the kemana, free desserts, and even two homework passes per year for the entirety of their high school career if they'd sign up, but not a single student had accepted. After a while she just gave up, realizing that it would just take time before anyone was comfortable enough to sign up. In reality, most magical beings weren't comfortable enough around each other, much less ready to integrate into a human-run military sector, and they *definitely* weren't prepared to allow their children to do so.

Luke rubbed his hands together and looked at the top of the steps as Ethan came barreling down in his Louper t-shirt. The back now read, Ethan for Captain. "Hey, man, you ready to learn what this game is all about?"

"Hell, yes! I've been ready all my life." Ethan laughed. "I just hope they take it kinda easy on me the first time around. I mean, I didn't try out for the team, and I don't have much of a clue about what I'm doing."

Luke chuckled and slapped him on the back. "I doubt they'll take it easy on you, but don't worry. They have a medic standing by."

11

It was the first Louper practice of the season, and everyone was stoked. All the new players minus Luke and Ethan showed up early dressed in their practice gear and ready to show the rest of the team what kind of talent they had. Luke and Ethan came running up, glad to see that the whole team wasn't there yet. The rest of the boys, the ones who had been on the team the year before, sauntered in waving to onlookers in the stands.

Max Regency, the head coach of the SNM Cardinals, trotted up in his cardinal-red jersey. It had an image of the bird on the front and his name across the back with a big "1" beneath it. The rest of the team's jerseys also had their names on the back, although their numbers were based on their seniority on the team. However, Regency didn't care about seniority. He cared about heart, ability, and motivation. He had noticed since tryouts that the returning players lacked all three of those things.

The old players sauntered in, waving at their friends,

and he clapped his hands and yelled at the spectators, "If you're not part of the team, get the hell off my field!"

The kids all groaned and threw their hands up before stomping out of the stands. The older boys rolled their eyes and got in line at the front of the group. Regency walked over and stood in front of them with a big smile on his face.

"I guess I'll start out the first practice by making it very clear that I don't care if you were on this team before. I don't care if you were a star player last year. Everyone on this team will begin at the same level, and how you perform, train, and build your character will determine what place you have in this organization."

The new players looked at each other with gleams of hope in their eye. Everyone wanted to be a starter. Everyone wanted to run out on that field with their names being called and the people in the stands cheering as loudly as they could for them. Luckily for them, they all had the motivation and the heart to climb to the top. The senior guys would be given a run for their money, but it didn't look like they cared. Regency nodded at his assistant, and the freshman tripped over his own feet as he handed Regency the clipboard.

"All right, guys, let's go over the basics, and I don't want to hear any groaning or moaning. Some of you need a refresher, some of you need an introduction, and some of you need to remember how the hell to play the game, because your head is too swollen for the headset you're gonna have to put on. Louper is played as a team. Let me repeat that for those of you who are listening—*Louper is played as a team*. At the beginning of every game, the chosen head of ceremony will cast a spell, and each of you will find yourselves in a different setting. Every game will be different. Each time you step on this field to start a new game, you will find yourself in a new setting. This setting is a virtual world—a magical spell that surrounds you, allowing you to see only that world while you're on the field.

"At first, this can be hard to maneuver through, especially since, depending on the field, what you're feeling isn't necessarily going to match up to what you are seeing. For example, you may find yourself in a swamp, stepping through bogs, seeing the water rise to your shins, and even smelling the stench of the water and algae. However, what you'll *feel* will be turf under your feet. You cannot allow yourself to be distracted by the difference between those two things. If you do, I can promise you your opponent will know, and will use that distraction to take you down."

The new guys looked at each other nervously. Many of them had played before, but never in a team setting, and never with the magic they would be spelled with. Regency nodded to his assistant and the kid ran over to the players, passing out handbooks with moving magical pictures on the covers. They were the rulebooks, thick, heavy, and containing everything they'd need to know to play the game. Regency was adamant that they needed to know the rulebook cover to cover if they wanted to have any chance of winning the game.

"Now, once you're in this virtual spell world, you will work as a team to get through the different obstacles and challenges, all the while facing off with your opponent. Often times you will find, especially at your age, that the players are evenly matched. However, don't let your guard down. There is always that one player who is far above and beyond anyone else on their team. They are the ones you have to watch out for. If a team member is defeated, they are out of the game. There will be no question about it, because the virtual world will disappear and you will find yourself in the center of the field. You'll be able to see your teammates, but they will no longer be able to see you. As far as they are concerned, you are dead and gone, at least until the end of the game."

Ethan scratched his head and tilted it to the side. "So, how do you win a game of Louper?"

Max Regency smiled and nodded. "That's a very good question, Ethan. I'll give you a pretty simple answer, although getting to that point is never as simple as it may seem. Whoever makes it to the end and retrieves the prize, trophy, or goal is the winner. Even if it's just one person from the team who makes it to the end, the entire team wins as a whole. You will receive a collection of coins that can be used in the closest kemana and a team trophy. Just to clarify, since there have been issues in the past about this, all prizes are split evenly among team members, no matter when they died during the game."

The guys whispered back and forth. They hadn't realized that they could win a prize like coins for the kemana. It was an extra bonus and motivation to ensure that they not only played as a team but that at least one of them made it to the end and retrieved what needed to be collected. Ethan was starting to understand why the coach insisted that it was a team effort. Without your teammates, there was nobody to protect you, fight alongside you, or make sure that someone, regardless of who it was, made it to the end.

Max nodded at Wyatt and waved him to the front. "Wyatt here is one of the best character developers I've ever met. He's going to explain to you exactly what you need to do to with your character to become one of the strongest players in the league."

Wyatt gave his usual charming smile and nodded at the guys as he stepped forward. "So, we all know we want to develop the strongest, smartest, and bravest player we can, but the big question is, how do we get there? Well, basically, whatever you are in reality—whether it's fit, smart, agile, fast—that's what you are in the game. So, if you work out in reality and get stronger, your character in the game gets stronger. If you study and get smarter, you're smarter in the game. Now, that all sounds like excellent motivation to get smarter and stronger in real life, but the one thing you have to keep in mind is that it's not just the good stuff that transfers to your character, it's the bad stuff, too. If you train too hard and get injured, your character will be injured in the game. If you stay up all night studying, partying, or any of the other things I know you guys do, your character is going to feel lethargic on the field. I don't know how it is for other guys, but when I walk out on that field already tired, I almost feel twice as tired when I step into my character."

Max Regency clapped his hands and waved his wand. "All right, boys, let's see what you got. Your first game is red versus blue."

The guys looked down at their shirts. Half had turned red, and half blue. Regency's magic changed from bright white to a green mist that circled them and floated into their noses and mouths. They stabilized themselves, blinked hard, and found themselves on the streets of New York City. The team had to search through abandoned subway tunnels and skyscrapers while keeping their eyes peeled for opponents.

Luke, although he hadn't played as much as the other boys, seemed to be a natural at the game. He swooped in and out, hiding from his opponents, taking them down, and protecting his teammates. He tried several times to save Ethan, but this was Ethan's first time playing the game, so he spent most of it getting demolished and then waiting on the sidelines for his next turn to go in.

Ethan didn't mind, though. He really liked the game, and couldn't wait to get better. He'd already decided he was going to recruit Luke to help him get stronger and smarter within the game, which would ultimately do that for him in real life, too.

Luke wasn't the one who found the trophy at the end, but he was still in the game when it was found, which was more than he had expected from his first day on the field. His team, the red team, managed to beat the blue team before they even knew where the trophy was. It didn't hurt that they had Wyatt on the team, but the coach was starting to see that Wyatt and Luke together made a pretty killer pair. When they returned to reality Max Regency clapped his hands, thinking the boys had worked better as a team than he'd initially thought they would.

"That was really good, guys. *Really* good. Who's up for another one?"

The guys all cheered, even Ethan, who felt a little bit

tired at that point. He knew he would never improve if he didn't continue to train, and he liked this Louper thing a lot more than he had thought he would. Max smiled and sent the green mist over them again. When they opened their eyes, they found themselves in a dense bayou surrounded by strange creatures, all out to get them. They ran for their virtual lives. The boys watched where they were stepping, trying not to sink into the mud as they attempted to cross the swamp.

It didn't take Luke and Wyatt long to realize that if they continued to be hampered by the mud, they would all be taken out within a matter of minutes. Wyatt stopped and looked at Luke, noting that he was on the same page. "All right, guys... If we want to get out of here alive with the trophy in our hands, we need to look up, not down. All these vines are strong and will hold our body weight. Start by pulling yourself out of the mud. You'll feel resistance, but remember that it's just a spell. It's not really there, so use your mind to lift yourself up and swing across until we can reach dry land. Are you in?"

All the guys reached for the vines, using their bodies' momentum to swing back and forth. As Luke swung forward and Wyatt nodded, he knew he'd found his place at the school, even if it were just for a couple of hours a day. Playing Louper, he was just like any other student.

12

"Can you sleep?" Izzie whispered, glancing at Alison, who was in the bed next to her. "I mean, I know you don't actually sleep, but are you tired? Or are you meditating?"

Alison chuckled and shook her head, turning toward Izzie, whose soul gleamed brightly in the bed next to her. "No, I'm not tired. I came back to the room during study hall and had a good session. I'd only been resting for days, so my body pretty much forced me into meditation. Right now, though, I'm wide-awake. Are you thinking what I'm thinking?"

"Time for a late-night stroll?" Izzie asked excitedly.

Alison sat up with a big smile and nodded. "I thought you were never going to ask!"

The girls quickly bundled up in the warmest clothes they could find. It was still February—the month where there is not only snow but everything iced over. Alison and Izzie were glad they had received new gloves and scarves for Christmas. While this winter didn't seem to be as bad as last year, once February hit the entire place iced over like a winter wonderland. The trees were encased in a layer of ice that sparkled and shimmered under the moonlight. The snow beneath their feet was hard and crunchy on top and it broke under each step, so they sank into the powder below. The wind that whipped across the fields was cold and bitter, but the girls didn't mind. They were just happy to be out on one of their walks. They had been busy lately, and Izzie had been exhausted after days of searching through her memories and thinking about all the things that had happened around her, so it had been a while since they'd taken a walk.

"Are you okay? I mean, after that day in class where you ran out?" Alison asked as they walked across the grounds.

Izzie shrugged and looked at the stars. "Yeah, I guess so. Something came back to me, and it was really confusing and took me off-guard. Seems like everything in my life is changing so fast, and I can't get a grip on it. My dreams are like memories and my memories are like dreams, and nothing seems to fit together anymore. I don't know... Maybe I'll never know the truth, but I have to at least try to figure it out."

Alison reached over and squeezed Izzie's hand, giving her a smile. "You need to do what is best for you. If finding out what happened in your past is best for you, then I support you completely."

Izzie squeezed her hand back. "I knew you would."

The girls walked up to the barn doors and squeezed inside, flipping on the lights. In the first stall was the gorgeous little colt that was born the year before. However, he wasn't as little as he used to be. He stood almost half as tall as his mother already. His coat was shiny, and his mane was fluffy on top of his head. As soon as he heard Izzie's voice, he ran to the stall door and rubbed his nose against Izzie's forehead. Izzie smiled and kissed him on the nose.

"You sure know how to make a girl feel special." She giggled, glancing at Alison.

The girls sat down carefully in the stall, and the colt and his mother laid down together in the straw. Izzie leaned back against the stall's wall.

"Are you ready for the Valentine's Day dance this year?"

"You know, I actually am. Last year's was a lot of fun, and I think this year's is gonna be even better. I like the dances because there's so much magic around me. The energy in the place is crazy, and I can see almost everything going on—not to mention everyone's excitement surging through their energy."

Izzie smiled. "On top of all of that, Luke has already asked me, and Tanner has already asked you. It's nice to be going to the dance with a date and not have to worry about someone asking you if you want to take a whirl on the dance floor. The first dance we went to, I was pretty sure I was going to be the wallflower nobody wanted to dance with."

Alison laughed and shook her head. "I would never let that happen. If no one else asked you to dance, you and I would have glided across the floor just like Ethan and Peter do every single year."

The girls giggled at the thought of Peter and Ethan

swirling across the floor, and Ethan dipping Peter. They always interrupted the romantic couples, but everyone else thought it was hilarious. Alison cleared her throat and tapped her fingers against her knee, glancing at the calming swirls moving through Izzie's energy.

"You know, Winter likes you."

Izzie scoffed. "Yeah, right. And why would you say something like that? This is the Valentine's Day dance, not Halloween, for God sakes. You're trying to give me nightmares."

Alison burst into laughter and shook her head. "I'm serious. He totally has a thing for you."

Izzie wrinkled her nose. "There is no way. He's from a dark family and goes out of his way to be mean to me. I'm pretty sure he would throw me to the wolves if he could, no pun intended."

Alison shrugged and watched the horses' energy. "He's only been that way half the time. The other half, he can't take his eyes off you. It's not only obvious to me, but to every single person who's around you guys. He stares at you like he's going to melt into the floor, and any time you're around Luke, it's like his heart is breaking. I would think it was romantic, except for the fact that he's covered in dark magic."

"*I* don't think it's romantic at all. You can't like someone and treat them like crap at the same time. Besides, Luke would eat him for dinner if he knew he had a thing for me. Boys are territorial, and on top of that, Luke is a shifter. Shifters take family very seriously. They are super-loyal. And by 'family,' I don't mean related by blood. It's anyone they truly care about."

Alison stood up laughing and lifted her hands. "Okay, okay. I wasn't suggesting you drop Luke and go to the other side. I was just letting you know what I saw in his soul when I watched the two of you."

Izzie laughed, but only halfheartedly. She hated the idea of Winter having feelings for her. He was part of a group of people who despised magical beings who weren't dark like them. On top of that, they had been responsible for the creation of the shifters. Luke was a shifter. Maybe not one created by the dark families, but definitely targeted by them. Whether Winter was a good guy or not, he'd never believe it until he stopped hanging out with the other dark magic beings.

Alison and Izzie turned out the lights and closed the barn door after them, then headed down the hill toward the edge of the forest where the dragon normally was. When they got there they whistled and called for him, but they didn't hear shuffling in the leaves like they normally did. Instead, a shadow flew over them, darkening the moon for a moment. Izzie looked up and watched as their dragon attempted to fly overhead. He wobbled back and forth as his wings flapped wildly, and his navigation was way off. He began to roll and lost altitude quickly, falling into a giant drift of snow several feet away from them.

The dragon poked his head out of the snow and tilted it to the side, staring lovingly at Alison and Izzie. Alison could see the wild swirling energy of the dragon and she giggled. He was up to something, most probably something mischievous. He'd tried to fly for days but had only been able to make it a short distance before tumbling to the ground.

"It looks like our little buddy's really getting good." Izzie laughed.

Alison looked at the energy trail overhead that led down to the dragon's soul. "It looks like he's only making it so far, but at least he's trying. There's really not a lot we can do to help teach him since we don't have wings."

Izzie sighed. "It would be freaking awesome if we could fly around campus. I would never get stuck in the hall next to Scarlett again."

The girls laughed, talking about all the things they would do if they could fly. They patted the dragon on the head and headed toward the back of the teachers' row where Horace's cabin was located. When they reached the top of the last hill, Izzie saw the glow from a small fire outside Horace's cabin. The girls clasped hands and raced down the hill, laughing and giggling and barely making it without falling face-first into the snow.

Horace sat next to the fire in his rickety old wooden chair with his golden retriever at his side. "Hey, girls, it's good to see you. I brought out two extra chairs just in case you showed tonight. It's a good thing I did."

Izzie smiled as she sat down next to Alison and patted the dog. "I'm glad you did. We always look for you when we're out."

Alison laughed and nodded. "It's true, although I think our rounds have gotten longer since the first time we walked the grounds at night. It's almost like we have a checklist of all the places we need to go now."

Horace chuckled and nodded as he warmed his hands by the fire. "Yeah, it usually happens that way."

Izzie rubbed her hands together and smiled at Horace. "Tell us a story, Horace. Something from long ago."

"Something from long ago, huh? Actually, I was told a story just this week. Apparently, thousands and thousands of years ago, right here in Charlottesville, giants used to walk these grounds."

Alison stared at Horace as his energy swirled around him. "Are you serious? Like *gigantic* giants used to walk these grounds?"

Horace nodded. "Apparently. I thought it was really interesting, and in fact, the tale is that the giants were the ones who carved out the lakes and streams in this area. Of course, that sounds more like a fairytale than reality, but at the same time, I live in a cabin in back of a magical school. I believe things now a little bit more easily than I used to."

The girls laughed and listened as Horace told other stories he'd heard from the professors about the history of the land the school was on. There were tales of magical creatures, wars, great loves, and everything in between. By the time he was done, both girls' eyes were heavy. They loved the stories, but the sun was about to come up, and they had class the next morning.

"You girls look like you're about to fall asleep right there in your chairs." Horace chuckled. "I won't take offense, or think it has anything to do with my storytelling abilities."

Izzie laughed, stood up, and brushed the fur off her pants. "Not at all. I loved hearing the stories, but I have to admit I'm pretty exhausted."

Alison stood up with Izzie and nodded, reaching out to

grasp Horace's hand. "I have to agree. I love the stories, but even *I'm* getting tired, and we have to go to class soon."

The girls said their goodbyes and headed toward the school. Izzie glanced over her shoulder one last time before walking into the foyer. She could imagine the giants making their homes on the grounds of the School of Necessary Magic.

13

That week, Ethan and several of the friends he had made between the Entrepreneur Club and the Louper team had worked in secret to build magical go-karts to race. When they had been completed and all the professors had gone to bed, the group set up a race track at the back of the estate, as far away from teachers' prying eyes as they could get. One of the seniors, a wizard who had met Ethan through the Louper team, stood at the edge of the field and cast a glamour over the event. Unless you were inside that perimeter, you'd never hear any of the noise from the go-karts or the cheering fans.

All of the go-karts had been magically decorated to represent the driver's grade, friends, and background. The whimsical cars mostly belonged to the Light Elves. The serious magical creations had been done by some of the older wizards and witches, and there were even race cars painted to look like shifters that had been created by their magical friends just for them. The only rules to join were: keep your mouth shut, be there on time, and don't tell anyone who would tell the professors. Ethan considered it one of his greatest achievements in school so far.

"All right, racers, take the line," one of the senior Light Elves called, putting her hand in the air. "Before we begin, let's go over the rules. Each track is magical. You will only be able to see a few feet in front of your cars, and the tracks will disappear behind you since that's way easier to hide from the teachers in case they catch us.

"Here are the race rules. There is absolutely no driving on anyone else's track, so stay in your own lane. We don't want to have any crazy crashes. All magic is legal, but you may only use it on your own cart. That means there will be no casting spells against anyone else, no matter how badly you want to win. If the rules are broken, that person will be disqualified from the race. The first one to circle the track five times will win bragging rights, and have the satisfaction of knowing he or she won the first race of the new go-kart extravaganza created by our very own Ethan."

Everyone cheered, and Ethan stood up in his go-kart and took a bow. Across the hills, sitting in his chair and patting his dog, Horace watched the students prepare to race. He wanted to make sure nothing went too far. The last thing he wanted was for one of them to get badly hurt doing something that they shouldn't be. Every year a new bunch of kids found some way to get themselves into trouble, and this year was no different. He sighed and shook his head, glancing at the trees behind the students. He turned the knob on his binoculars and focused on the silver dragon watching from a tree branch high above the fray.

The branch was bending toward the ground. He could imagine creaks and cracks each time the dragon moved. He had gotten much bigger since the last time Horace had seen him, and that had only been a few weeks ago. Given what the creature was eating, it wasn't exactly a surprise. In fact, as the dragon watched the kids, he was busy having a late-night snack.

Horace patted his dog. "Looks like it's going to be an exciting evening, huh, boy?"

The dog whined and laid his snout between his front legs. Horace watched as the go-karts lined up perfectly, no vehicle even a centimeter in front of the others. He couldn't hear what was being said, but he could tell that the girl up front was explaining the rules. Some of the students nodded in understanding while others rolled their eyes and chuckled, obviously not planning to follow the rules. Horace had no idea why they thought this would be a good idea, especially with so much animosity between the magicals, the shifters, and the dark kids. It was a stupid idea, but what was he going to do? It was just a bunch of teenagers having fun.

Scanning the crowd from the center out, Horace noticed Izzie and Alison, out on one of their usual late-night strolls, hanging back and watching the action from the shadows. It looked like Izzie was giving Alison a play-by-play of all the different go-karts and drivers on the track. Horace bit the inside of his lip and looked down at his dog, then glanced back up at the ever-growing crowd. He was starting to think that he should send his dog to warn the headmistress. The last thing he wanted was for someone to get injured, and it was very likely to happen.

However, before he decided, it was too late. One of the senior female Light Elves stepped out in front of the cars wearing a short skirt, knee-high socks, and Mary Janes and raised her hands. In her palm, a fireball began to simmer, growing larger and larger until it filled her whole hand. The crowd counted down with her. "Five...four... three...two..."

As the girl yelled, "Go," she tossed the fireball straight up, and it exploded into sparks like a firework. Because of the protection spell they had placed around the track Horace couldn't hear the explosion, but he could definitely see it. The go-karts took off at blinding speed, each racing down their own personal track. Dust flew up, and everyone pointed and laughed loudly as the drivers attempted to get ahead of each other.

Horace leaned forward as the woods lit up in a succession of bright headlights and even brighter taillights. On the track, Ethan gripped the steering wheel tightly as the trees disappeared and then reappeared behind him, not standing in the way of his go-kart. Ethan's heart pounded furiously as he raced around the course. Faces whizzed by watching and cheering the different drivers on. He blinked and focused on the three feet of track he could see in front of him, then jerked the steering wheel to the left when he realized he was close to nicking a driver next to him. His breath caught in his throat as he skidded past, his chest struggling to rise and fall as he sped forward.

"Lead the pack," Ethan whispered to himself, finding his car in the lead but only for a moment's time. One of the dark wizard kids narrowed his eyes and pulled his wand from the seat next to him, then flicked his wrist and sent out a dark spray of magic, the sparks almost too dark to see. The magic hit Ethan's wheels and sent him spinning in circles, barely missing the other cars before he skidded to a stop and stalled.

Ethan slammed his fist on the steering wheel as the dark wizard flew past with a smirk on his face. He couldn't believe that he had been in the lead just minutes before, and now he'd lost the race. The rules were there for a purpose, and even though Ethan wasn't one to follow the rules on a normal basis, he wasn't happy that he had been bested at his own game. He took off his seatbelt and stepped out to protest the dark wizard's magic, but he froze in his tracks.

Beyond the opening to the woods, the Headmistress and Professor Hudson came barreling over the hill headed straight for them. Shouts arose from the crowd, and everyone scattered in different directions. The older students quickly shrank their cars to matchbox size, scooping them up and shoved them in their pockets before bolting. Ethan pulled out his wand and twisted it. His first attempt increased the size of the go-kart and he cursed under his breath, trying to get the spell correct. He flicked and fluttered as the headmistress got closer. Panic started to set in.

After several tries, Ethan got the car to shrink down small enough for him to grab it and take off at a sprint. From a few hills over, Alison turned her hands palms up and sent out a dark shadow that rushed across the grounds, giving Ethan enough cover to dash back to his dorm without getting caught. Izzie looked at Alison with surprise, but she wasn't completely shocked. Alison was loyal to her friends, even when they were breaking the rules.

Professor Hudson grabbed the headmistress' arm while using her wand to cut through the darkness. "Only a Drow has that kind of magic, and we only have one Drow at the school. Those two girls have very powerful magic. If they ever learn how to use their magic together..."

Headmistress Berens shook her head. "Isn't the point of them being here that they learn to work together?"

Without another word she turned, not wanting to waste time searching through the dark for students who might still be out there. She knew the ones responsible were already back at the dorms. Alison had made sure they got away safely. She charged through the courtyard and into the mansion. In her office, she shut and locked the door, grabbed the box off the shelf, and sat down at her desk. She waved her wand over the box and waited for the latches to disconnect before tilting back the lid.

Inside, an even larger number of black dots covered the glowing balls of light. The headmistress had no way to stop what might be coming, not that she understood what it was. She dreaded the consequences of having removed Izzie's memories. She closed the lid and leaned forward on her elbows, rubbing the exhaustion from her face. She couldn't help but think that it had been a mistake to allow the dark families' children to attend the school. They were just kids, though, and she hoped that encouragement from the staff and being surrounded by light magic would leave a lasting impression on them. Besides, either the kids had to learn to work together, or they would continue to try to kill each other off in the future.

Headmistress Berens knew that somebody had to step forward. Someone had to stand up for both the kids and the future of magical beings, and what better way than to start when they were young? She hoped her actions would lead to a better future, but there was still that lingering feeling that she just might've made the wrong choice. At this point, all she could do was wait and see.

14

I zzie clutched Luke's hand as they followed Alison and Tanner down the stairs to the foyer. Both Alison and Izzie lifted the fronts of their dresses enough not to trip on the red fabric that flowed to the floor. Izzie's was long with a full skirt. Alison's was more fitted, rolling down her curves and gently touching the floor. Kathleen had pulled their hair back, letting wisps of small curls dangle around their faces, especially Alison's. Her silver hair shimmered under the lights. Tanner and Luke were dressed in perfectly-tailored suits with red vests and shiny dress shoes. Tanner's tie was a red sequined fabric, while Luke wore a bowtie with hearts on it. Both young men looked sleek while remaining true to their personalities.

They walked through the entrance of the cafeteria, which had been transformed for the romantic Valentine's soirée. On every table and lining the walls were bunches of roses that Horace had spent the long winter perfecting in the greenhouses on the grounds. The ceiling was enchanted to look like it was sunset, except instead of oranges and reds the clouds were misty pink, and the light changed appropriately as it got later. The floor shimmered and sparkled in metallic shades of pink and red, and as girls walked onto it, tiny hearts fluttered up around their ankles. The DJ was situated on the platform as usual, and a bright red dance floor had been magicked in place.

The hall was already crowded, teeming with students excited to show off their clothing and their dates and having a good time with their friends. Ethan had finally convinced Grace to come with him. Kathleen had agreed to be Peter's date, and Aya and Emma had arrived with a couple of upperclassmen. Alison, Izzie, Tanner, and Luke walked up and greeted their friends.

"Aya, I didn't know you had a date," Izzie whispered curiously.

Aya shook her head. "No, no, it's not what you think it is. Emma's date needed a date for his best friend. We're just here as friends. He knows I have a boyfriend back at home."

Izzie nodded in understanding and squeezed Aya's hand. "That's really sweet of you. Don't be nervous, just have a good time. We are all here as friends."

Aya nodded and looked a bit relieved. Kathleen and Peter walked up with Ethan and Grace in tow and hugged the others, excited to see them. Before they had a chance to talk music blasted out of the speakers, signifying the start of the dance. Tanner twirled Alison onto the dance floor, holding her close and taking the moment to spend some time with her. Luke and Izzie danced with the others and laughed wildly at Ethan's and Peter's crazy moves. They were surprised but pleased when Grace jumped in. She was goofy, not like the others had imagined, and she fit in perfectly with them.

After five songs, everybody was breathing heavily and sweating. Luke leaned over and kissed Izzie on the cheek. "Going to grab something to drink."

Izzie nodded and smiled. "I'll be right here waiting for you."

Izzie smiled as Luke walked away. She went over to Alison and grabbed her hand, not saying a word but just letting her know she was there. Alison used this break to pick out the souls of the people she knew and tried to remember some that were new. She could see many different souls in the room, but also the darkness in many of them. She noted how almost everyone with dark magic inside them congregated, moving away from the light magic as if it repelled them.

"Here you go." Luke smiled and handed out the cups of punch he'd brought back from the refreshment stand.

Alison smiled in thanks and took a sip, but set it down on the table next to her. There was a strange taste to it that she couldn't put her finger on. Izzie sipped hers as well and put it down, but Luke gulped his in two swallows. He let out a deep breath, wiped his hand across his lips, and gave her a big toothy grin, then cleared his throat and tapped his fist against his chest as if he had swallowed the punch wrong. He shook his head and smiled again, holding his hand out to Izzie. When she accepted, he pulled her back out onto the dance floor. She laughed, rolling into his arms as they danced wildly across the floor to the music.

He spun her, releasing one hand and twirling her in front of him. Luke couldn't remember the last time he'd had such a great time, which was saying a lot considering the year he'd had. He'd made the Louper team, given Izzie her first kiss, and spent every day since winter break feeling as if he were actually part of the magical community for the first time in his life. It was a high he couldn't explain.

After a moment, though, Luke started to feel a bit woozy. He touched his forehead and closed his eyes as the room spun, then opened his eyes and looked at Izzie, who was smiling and dancing in front of him. She went from beautiful to blurry in about three seconds. He shook his head and blinked to try to focus, but nothing he did worked. The room was still spinning and he wobbled, slightly concerned that he might pass out right there.

Izzie put her hand on his arm, realizing that something was wrong. "Luke, are you okay? You look really pale, and you just started sweating out of nowhere. Why don't you sit down?"

Izzie tried to lead him off the dance floor, but he shook his head and pulled back, realizing that he knew exactly what he was experiencing. He hadn't expected this. He'd spent years as a child controlling his urges to shift, but at that moment, it was like his control had been stripped away. He wasn't sure he could hold back much longer.

"Something's wrong," he muttered, pushing Izzie to the side to protect her. "I need you to stay here. Don't follow me. It could be dangerous. Something's just not right."

Before Izzie could say anything, Luke bounded out the door in a hasty exit. He wanted to lose Izzie before she could follow him. He rammed his way through the other students, knocking over several vases of flowers, and sprinted outside. He didn't stop once he reached the steps. He kept going, heading toward the woods as fast as he possibly could. With each step, he took off a piece of his clothing. First his tie, then his jacket, and finally his shirt. He balled them up in his hands and threw them behind the bushes, hoping he'd remembered where they were whenever what was happening had run its course.

As he raced toward the woods, he saw Farrell doing the same thing across the field. Farrell's eyes were bright amber, and fur had already started to sprout from his neck, his arms, and the backs of his hands. Luke could feel the same thing happening to him. The blunt edges of his teeth transformed into the sharp fangs of his wolf. His heart pounded, not because of the change, but because he knew that it wasn't just him. He wasn't the only one who had lost control of his ability. There was something seriously wrong going on, and he immediately feared that the wolves were under attack.

When he reached the edge of the woods, he let the change take him. He was no longer able to fight it off, and he knew he would be able to think better once he had shifted. His feet changed to paws, and his bones shifted and cracked as he morphed into the wolf he had become so comfortable as. Once the change was complete, he stopped in a pile of crisp leaves. He heard Izzie's breathing all the way across the fields and he turned his head back, focusing his bright amber eyes on the beautiful girl in the red dress as she ran through the doorway and scanned the courtyard and fields in fright.

All he had ever wanted to do was protect her, and what happened? He ended up losing control at the school dance with her in his arms. It could have gone really badly, especially with all the dark kids just waiting for a chance to attack one of the shifters. He could never have let anything happen to Izzie, no matter what it did to him.

Izzie panicked, watching Luke jet out of the room with that familiar yellow tint to his eyes and a wild look on his face. She had seen his wolf before. Luke was changing, and it didn't seem like he had any control over it. That wasn't like him, so she knew something was wrong.

Izzie refused to be pushed aside. She was much tougher than that, and she wasn't going to just sit by and wait until Luke came back—*if* he came back. She held her dress up as she ran across the foyer and down the steps into the courtyard. She stopped and looked left and right, narrowing her eyes as she saw a wolf leap into the woods. She started to hurry across the courtyard but stopped when Tanner grabbed her arm.

"Izzie, it's not safe. If Luke wanted you to stay back, it was for your protection. There is obviously something going on. Stay here. We'll get the Headmistress. She should have an idea of what to do at this point."

Izzie shook her head, not wanting to hear it. She wasn't going to let Luke disappear like that. Something had forced him to change, something dark. She could feel it in her chest. It pulled at her as if it searched for the light inside her. She thrust her energy out to shove Tanner back. He was surprised by the amount of power she'd produced and was unable to keep his feet, falling on his butt and bouncing. It knocked the wind out of him, and for a moment Izzie stared at him, shocked. He knew she'd done it on purpose, and he waved his hand to let her know he was okay.

Tears filled her eyes, but she couldn't let him distract her. She pulled off her shoes and raced toward the woods, determined to find Luke and figure out what in the world was going on. It was freezing outside and there was still light snow covering the ground, but Izzie didn't care. She couldn't even feel the cold against her feet. She bolted across the ridgeline to the edge of the forest, skidded to a stop where the shadows met the light of the moon, and searched the woods in front of her.

She turned to her right and walked along the tree line, hoping that she'd catch a glimpse of him, coax him out, and help him turn back into his human form. She tripped over something and looked down at one of Luke's shoes. Izzie grabbed the shoe, holding in her front of her before clutching it to her chest. She shook her head and looked deep into the forest.

"Luke," she whispered.

15

Headmistress Berens closed the conference room's doors and turned back to the group of teachers who had gathered. Some of them had been at the dance and had seen what happened, while others had been summoned from their cottages at the bottom of the hill to discuss the situation. There was a loud murmur among the teachers, and fear floated through the room. The headmistress sat down at the head of the table, clutching her hands together and pressing them to her lips. She was trying not to let fear take her over while she was figuring out what had happened.

"Someone poisoned the shifters," Professor Hudson announced loudly, quieting the group.

For the next several moments, you could have heard a pin drop in the room. No one wanted to say it, but it was true. Someone or something had managed to turn all the shifters into their wolves, destroying any control they might have had over the change. Headmistress Berens had seen it before, but it had been twenty years since anything like that had happened. The rest of the teachers took seats and stared at the headmistress.

"We have to keep our wits about us," she stated calmly. "This is a very serious situation, and it needs our full attention, without emotion or fear driving us. If you need to take a moment, do so, but this discussion must be focused."

Professor Hodges peered at the others, wanting to speak up but nervous about what they might think. After a few moments of contemplation, he realized he was one of the best people to say something. He cleared his throat and took a deep breath.

"It's obvious that the first thing we need to do, beyond making sure that all the shifters in the school are safe, is figure out who was behind it. This wasn't a random occurrence. It wasn't something induced by the moon or even a spell. We would have sensed that type of spell, and all shifters, including the professors, would've been affected by it."

The door creaked open, and Horace entered carrying a cup of punch from the dance. He set it down in front of the headmistress and whispered into her ear. She looked at the ceiling and back down at the cup, then pulled out her wand and waved it over the top. As the curls of magic swirled through the liquid in the cup, the bright red punch turned black.

"Well, I guess we know what happened." The headmistress sighed and put away her wand.

"I think it's obvious who was responsible for this. For a very long time, the dark families have waged war with the shifters. I don't think it's a coincidence that when we allowed their children to attend this school, there's suddenly an issue where shifter students can't control their inner wolves." The librarian clenched his fist. The poppy on his hat was eerily still.

The teachers began to talk excitedly again, and Headmistress Berens put up a hand to hush them. "All right, everyone, calm down. Yes, there might be an issue with the dark children, but it's not something we can jump to conclusions about without any evidence or basis. As the heads of the school, we're responsible for investigating every possible avenue before pinning something like this on a group of kids. If we are not absolutely certain that the dark families' children are behind this, it could cause an enormous problem between the dark families and the light magicals, not just in the school but outside of it as well."

"I agree," Hodges replied. "I think that that's too easy of an answer. I'm not saying it shouldn't be explored, but I think that whoever did this was smarter than just a group of dark magic kids playing a prank. The headmistress is correct. We need to investigate every avenue."

"What about the parents? If they find out about this, there is going to be some serious trouble. Not just with the school or us, but with the government. They will draw their own conclusions, and it could start a serious battle between the dark and the light. That cannot be allowed to happen." Professor Regency looked worried, not just for the students, but for everyone.

Headmistress Berens nodded, and quietly contemplated the situation. Professor Regency was correct. Before this news got out to the parents, they would have to come up with an explanation. They needed to know who was responsible for it so that the correct people were punished for what they had done. Otherwise, threats would be thrown, old feuds would be sparked, and the results could be dire for the magical community.

"Good, then let's keep it to ourselves until we know more."

The next day was strange, not just for the students, but the teachers as well. There was a peculiar feeling flowing through the halls of the school, and while not everyone had witnessed what had happened, enough rumors were flying to fill in the gaps.

When the students filed into transfiguration class with Professor Hodges his outward appearance was as calm and professional as it usually was, but he wasn't wearing his normal bright, shiny smile. On the inside, it was a different story. He felt utterly shaken up and exhausted from the events of the weekend, but the children were there to learn. He needed to keep the atmosphere as normal as possible, so he did his best to hide his mood and disguise his exhaustion.

"Good morning, class. I know some of you are struggling right now, but I would like to ask that we all try to focus and learn something new. Today, we're going to learn how to transfigure common objects. Basically, this is shifter magic."

A wave of whispers blew over the class and the professor waited until everyone had quieted down, knowing that getting angry with them or shutting them down would only spark more dissent. Once they were quiet, he took the time to explain the spell and had several of the students demonstrate for the class. When the students were done, everyone prepared to practice the spell at their desks. Large wooden blocks were placed in front of each student, and everyone pulled out their wands or used their inner light magic trying to turn the block into a toy, a vase, a pen, or any other common object they could think of.

Alison ran her fingers over the wood, feeling the grain beneath her fingers. She closed her eyes and pulled her energy up through her chest and down her arms, feeling the heat race through her. She lightly touched the grained surface, letting the magic flow out of her and cover it like a blanket. The woodblock shimmered under her magic, growing brighter and brighter until finally, it transformed into a metal toaster. It was leaps and bounds above what the other students were able to achieve, and the professor couldn't help but notice.

Professor Hodges walked over to Alison and laid his hand on her shoulder. In his energy, she noticed the tired strands of blue and gray swirling and mixing with the colors of worry and distress he'd tried to hide. It was hard for him to do so, though, since he was incapable of the kind of magic everyone else could do. He leaned down and whispered to her.

"Come with me to the side of the room. I want to talk to you about something."

Alison nodded and followed the professor across the class into the corner. Only Izzie and Kathleen noticed, but since she wasn't being led from the classroom, they returned to their spells. The professor cleared his throat and began to talk, hoping he wasn't overstepping.

"You are a natural at this. You just don't know it yet."

Alison lifted an eyebrow and narrowed her eyes. "I don't understand."

"Drow can take on the appearance of others. I'm not sure if you knew that."

Alison shook her head. "I'm trying to learn as much about them as I can, but I didn't know that."

"They can't become a different species, but they can take on anyone's appearance and look completely different. They've used this in the past to fool even those who knew them the best. Apparently, Drow magic is so powerful they can even fool their own mother. There isn't any spell required for it, at least from what I know. It's more about confidence or need. When you really need to do something, the Drow magic will take over and allow you to transform into someone else."

Alison looked at him like he was crazy. She wasn't sure why he was telling her this, but she found it very interesting. She hadn't read about that ability anywhere, but she wasn't surprised. Not many people knew anything about Drow magic, and she was honestly a bit taken back that Professor Hodges did. If she had known, she would have come to him sooner, but at the same time, she wasn't sure what it would've done for her.

"The need?" Alison tilted her head to the side, not quite sure what he meant.

"Sure. Like when you threw the shadows over the go-kart races. I mean, I'm guessing that was you. No need to confirm. I hadn't seen you do that before, but I just have to say you did it really well. And I can almost bet that you did it without any preparation or using any energy."

Alison looked from right to left before nodding. He smirked and patted her on the shoulder, letting her know that she wasn't in any trouble. He just wanted to talk to her about it, to explain to her what need was. She had probably experienced it a million times in her life, but she had never truly understood the difference between casting a spell and letting her magic work through her. It hadn't been a shock to him when he'd found out her mother was a Drow princess, which made her a princess in her own right. Of course, on Earth that didn't carry the same weight as it would on their home planet, but it *did* mean that she was full of strong and powerful magic that went deeper than almost anybody at that school could understand.

"See? You had a need. Why don't you give it a try? Focus. Think of a visual attribute of a person, like your silver hair for example. Try to change your silver hair to whatever color you deem appropriate. If it works, you should be able to see the energy change."

Alison took a deep breath and nodded, figuring it was worth a try. She closed her eyes and focused inward, remembering the energies that had flown around her mother and what that told her about herself. She then compared that to Izzie's soul and Izzie's energy, trying to change herself into what she pictured Izzie looked like. The magic flowed over her and light gleamed all over her body, twisting around her arms like vines, and up her legs and across her stomach. Sections of Alison's silver hair sparkled and shimmered, changing from brown to blonde to red and finally back to silver.

Feeling the intensity of her effort, she let out a deep breath and released the magic back into her chest. What she'd attempted was hard. Even harder when she wasn't sure what she should have been picturing. She opened her eyes and looked at the excitement flowing through the professor's energy. He squeezed her shoulder.

"It'll come. You're very clever. Give it time. And besides, you're a teenager—drama always turns up. I'm pretty sure you'll experience the need sooner rather than later."

16

Professor Lucy Fowler stood at the front of the Plants for Potions class, nervously tapping her fingers on the desk. She was lost in her thoughts. She was dressed as crazily as usual, in a knee-length quilted skirt, a bright yellow top, and a knitted cardigan with cats in berets on the back. Her bright yellow tights matched her top, and her boots had small jingling balls attached to the back. Her wild, frizzy red hair stuck out everywhere, untamed.

Professor Fowler had decided to change the class structure for that day. She thought that teaching the students about using herbs to make a healing potion might be more useful, especially in these times, than creating a potion to improve one's complexion. Not every student agreed with her, especially Kathleen, who was sitting in the back pouting. She'd waited all year to learn that potion. Still, after the events of the last two years, Professor Fowler had become concerned for the safety and well-being of the students around her.

"Good morning, class. For those who were expecting the complexion potion today, I apologize. I've changed the lesson plan. I think you should know how to use herbs to create a healing potion. We will learn how to create the complexion potion before the end of the year, but I promise you that at least one person in this class will be thankful at some point that they learned the ancient art of using herbs to heal."

The students looked at each other, wondering if the change had anything to do with the recent events. Not everyone knew the details of what had happened, but it had been enough to scare many of them. Surprisingly, though, it wasn't necessarily because they didn't feel safe with the shifters, but more because they knew someone in their midst was putting other students in danger. No one wanted to be the next one on their list. Anyone with light magic would've scoffed at the idea of harming the shifters, which meant that whoever was behind it most likely dabbled in dark magic. People like that never stopped at just the shifters.

"Most of the plants you see in front of you were collected on Oriceran, something I did on my last trip to the planet. The instructions are in your text, and if anyone has any questions, just raise your hand, and I'll come right over. All the plants are labeled, but please memorize what they look like. That way, if you want to make this potion in the future and you take a trip to Oriceran, you'll have no trouble finding them."

The students got to work, whispering to each other happily as they crushed the different herbs and added them to the various extracts and fluids boiling in small black pots on Bunsen burners in front of them. Aya used the tongs to carefully lift a vial of liquid and used her other hand to adjust her goggles. As she turned, she clipped the edge of the pot and dropped the potion onto the counter. The glass vial shattered and the liquid turned to dust, pluming up around Izzie. Before she realized what happened, Izzie took a deep breath and coughed.

She took off her goggles and rubbed her eyes, realizing that she had just inhaled the potion. She turned to look at Aya, but she found that she was no longer inside the classroom. Instead, she was in the midst of a great battle. She dropped her goggles and turned quickly when a stream of dark magic whizzed by her face. The beautiful woman with the long dark hair that she had seen in her dreams stood next to the man with the long silver hair. She felt longing in her heart as soon as she saw the two of them, but she still had no idea who they were.

Izzie struggled to understand what was going on as she watched the two of them send blasts down a long dark alley. Another burst of dark magic flew past her, whipping up her hair. She had thought it was just a dream, but that felt all too real. She spun to face the wizards at the other end of the alley, who wore dark cloaks pulled up over their heads and sent out dangerous bursts of black magic with every twist of their wands.

She tilted her head to the side and stared at the faces of the dark wizards as they battled with the woman and man she'd grown so attached to. The dark magicals were so angry and determined that she was instinctively inclined to fight them. Without thinking, she thrust out her arms and pulled energy from the ground into her chest. Her hair blew wildly around her in what she thought was the alleyway, but in reality, she was still standing in front of her Bunsen burner. To everyone in the classroom, she was simply frozen in place. Her eyes glowed brightly, lighting up the entire classroom.

Izzie screamed, and the energy in her chest rolled down her arms and out of her fingertips. The light that emanated from her body was so bright that everyone shielded, then the energy pulsed through the room and threw them to the floor. A large orb of fire burst from her chest, shattered desks all the way across the room, and rolled straight at Professor Fowler. The professor dove to the ground behind her desk and covered her head. She felt the heat when the orb whirled past her, and it blew a hole straight through the back of the classroom.

Some of the elves jumped to their feet to hurry to Izzie's side. The symbols on her arms, upper chest, and neck flipped so fast that no one could read them before they disappeared. Light glimmered all over her body, and though her eyes were open, she wasn't aware of the classroom. Izzie was in the alley—a place she had seen many times in her dreams. It was the nightmare she woke up from night after night with sweat pouring from her forehead. This time, though, she was able to look around, and it didn't feel like a dream or memory. It felt like she was really there. Like she could reach out and touch the people around her, and more importantly, like the magic flying at her head could do damage.

Alison sat on the floor, watching as the colors of Izzie's

energy changed and swirled. There was fear, there was curiosity, and there was more than enough rage to have created that massive hole in the back of the classroom. Although Alison couldn't see the expression on Izzie's face, she could tell that Izzie wasn't in the classroom—at least not in her mind. Luckily, Alison wasn't the only one who noticed. Professor Fowler jumped up and ran over her to her cabinet, frantically pulling out a number of jars and dropping them on the counter. She pulled out the mortar and pestle and mumbled to herself as she shook herbs into the round stone bowl. She used the pestle to crush them as fast as she possibly could, then mixed them with her wand.

When Professor Fowler was finished, she grabbed a palmful of the herbs and whispered quietly over them, sending a light layer of magic into the plants. She ran to Izzie, pulled her jaw down, and shoved the herbs into her mouth. Almost instantly, the visions began to subside, and the haze over Izzie's pupils dissipated, leaving them their normal blue hue. Izzie shook her head and blinked, then glanced at the students on the floor. Confusion took over her face as she looked at Professor Fowler, who was breathing heavily and leaning against the counter.

The disorientation that Izzie was feeling and the confusion that plagued her started to float away as she turned in a circle staring, at all the students peeking up over their desks. "I... I... What's going on?"

Izzie looked at Aya, who slowly pointed to the giant hole in the back wall of the classroom. Izzie shook her head and put her hands to her mouth, not understanding fully that she'd created the smoking hole and caused the surprised looks on the student's faces. She had let go of her control, and although it wasn't her fault, she couldn't help but imagine that she could have killed someone.

Professor Fowler asked Kathleen and Emma to escort Izzie back to her dorm room to get cleaned up and rested after what had happened. She had explained to Izzie that she had inhaled some powerful herbs by accident and halluci-nated. What she didn't tell the girl was exactly what had happened. When the girls were gone, Professor Fowler cast a spell to sweep up all the glass and clean up all the herbs and leftover potions. She gave the class free time until the bell rang, and turned toward the giant hole in the wall. She lifted an eyebrow. It would take a bit more than a swish of her wand to fix it.

"Aya, please find Professor Powell and tell him I need him in the potions lab. There's a bit of a mess to clean up, and I don't think I can handle this one on my own. It might take a couple of hands."

Alison raised her hand, and Professor Fowler called her name. "Professor, if you'd like, I can probably handle fixing that wall."

The professor shook her head and chuckled. "Thank you, Alison, but I think we've had enough student magic for the day. We will leave this one to the professionals."

Aya returned right before the bell and let Professor Fowler know that she couldn't find Professor Powell, but she'd been told he was probably in the gardens taking a break between classes. Professor Fowler nodded and thanked Aya for the attempt, then grabbed her wand and headed out of the classroom before any of the students had left. She walked down the hall to the doors leading out to the garden and found Professor Powell standing in front of the ancient tree, taking a moment to himself.

"Professor Fowler," he said without turning around. "What can I do for you?"

"I'm sorry to disturb you, but I have a bit of a mess in my room. Izzie accidentally inhaled some rare, powerful herbs, and unfortunately went into a vision, where I am assuming she was in some sort of battle."

Professor Powell opened his eyes and stared at the tree. "Is everyone all right?"

"Fortunately, everyone is fine." She took a step toward Professor Powell and clasped her hands together, lowering her voice. "Did you know that Izzie is a Jasper Elf? A Jasper Elf! She almost took out half the classroom today, and she wasn't even trying. She was in the middle of the vision. I've never had magic like that used in front of me before. Of course, she wouldn't have meant to, but she could have easily killed the entire class with the amount of power behind the magic that shot out of her. You should've seen the symbols on her body. They flipped over so fast that no one could read them. What do we do?"

"Nothing," Professor Powell snapped as he swung around to stare at Professor Fowler. "We mind our own business."

Professor Fowler could see that she had upset Powell, so she backed away quickly and returned to her classroom. After she was gone, however, Professor Powell slowly walked back through the halls of the school with a look of concern on his face. He crept to Professor Fowler's classroom and stared at the hole with wide eyes, then hurried through hordes of students goofing around in the halls and barked orders at them.

"Break it up. Get to your next appointments before I put you all in detention!"

17

"Get down, get down!" Wyatt yelled, waving his arm over his head and ducking behind a boulder.

The boys were at another Louper practice, battling it out on a mountainside on Oriceran this time. Many of them had never seen Oriceran before, and they struggled to stay focused on the game when there were so many things around them that they'd been curious about for years. Coach Regency tried to be understanding. He'd found that his first-year players got stuck on the Oriceran virtual fight more than any other.

Coach Regency cast a spell on himself and floated through the scene, watching how they interacted and taking note of where they needed more training. However, he started to think this wasn't the right battle for him to monitor. He should probably pick something easier, like the streets of post-apocalyptic Chicago or deep below the ocean in Atlantis—one of his favorites, mostly because of the mermaids.

"Come on, boys, don't get distracted! I know you've

never seen Oriceran before, but if you just focus on this fight and get through it, I can spell you all back here so you can explore a little bit. You're not going to get to see anything when those dragons attack and burn you to a crisp."

Coach Regency groaned, rubbed his small hands over his face, and took a deep breath. He watched as several of his players were eaten in one fell swoop as the dragon flew by the mountainside. Its claws battered several others, and they tumbled to their deaths on the rocky ground below. Those students found themselves back on the field, bummed that they were no longer on Oriceran.

"Your opponent will use your sightseeing to their advantage," Coach Regency yelled. "Think about it: if you are in a game with another team and half the team wandered around smelling the roses and looking off into the sunset, what would you do? You would use it to your advantage. You would take out the whole damn team in one fell swoop with a giant dragon! So if you don't want to find yourself dreaming of the sunset on another planet as thick, sharp claws grab you and drop you to your death, I would suggest put away your childish desire to explore Oriceran right now and focus on the damn game!"

Luke chuckled as he climbed over a boulder and kicked a zombie off the side of the mountain. He kept running. He was doing pretty well, especially given the fact that he lacked motivation after the whole Valentine's Day event. When he rounded the corner, Henry stuck his foot out from behind a rock and tripped him while Wyatt tackled him to the ground and laughed.

"You gonna play with the big boys, you have to learn how to pay attention to the details."

Luke grumbled and pushed Wyatt off. "It's not like I've been here before. This is all foreign territory, and I don't need my teammates tripping me in the middle of it."

Wyatt chuckled and shrugged. "I've been to Oriceran, and I've seen this mountain before. In fact, I'm pretty sure my father has climbed this mountain. Of course, he wasn't facing zombie attacks, dragons, or crazy dark wizards hiding around every corner. His goal was just to reach the top, which he did. Actually, this mountain is right on the edge of the Dark Forest, and I am pretty sure I heard The Gardener in the distance."

Coach Regency smacked Wyatt on the back of his head. "Come on, boys, keep your heads in the game!"

They went back to playing. One by one everyone was eliminated, and Henry found himself at the top of the mountain collecting his trophy.

Izzie looked in the mirror and smoothed down the flyaway hairs that hadn't made it into her tight ponytail. She wiped off the excess eyeliner that she had accidentally smudged. She wanted to look her best for the next rehearsal of *The Wizard of Oz*. For some reason, she felt like she needed to look pretty to play Dorothy. She knew it was dumb that it made her feel good, but she put the makeup on anyway.

When she was satisfied with her appearance, she pulled her foot up on the bed and tightened her Chuck Taylors. She grabbed her jacket just in case and headed out of the dorm room, smiling at the girls in the common area. For the first time in a while, no one seemed stressed. They were watching movies, studying, or gathered in a group whispering and giggling about whatever was going on in their lives. Izzie thought about how nice it was that for just one moment everything seemed normal, or at least what she understood normal was supposed to be like.

"Hey, Izzie," one of the girls said, waving at her.

"Hey," Izzie replied in a friendly voice.

"You heading to the rehearsal? I can't wait until the play. I already bought my tickets."

"Yeah." She chuckled. "I'm glad to hear it. It's going to be a really great show."

Although Izzie was happy that people were buying tickets, she was also really nervous. She had never performed in front of a bunch of people before, or at least she didn't think she had. This was her stage debut, and Dorothy had been her favorite character growing up, the same as every other girl at the orphanage. Maybe it was because Dorothy had escaped the trauma and found herself in a beautiful new world, something all the girls wished for even if Izzie couldn't actually remember the girls wishing for anything —or the girls, for that matter.

As she walked toward the auditorium, she passed the Entrepreneur Club meeting. She slowed down for a moment when Grace received a round of applause for her invention. Izzie couldn't help but be proud of her. Next door to that was the Future Leaders Club, which Izzie tried to avoid at all costs. They were holding a special meeting that day to discuss the elections and decide who they were voting for, if they weren't running themselves. The elections were a serious matter to them, even though Izzie thought it was ridiculous.

When Izzie walked through the auditorium doors, Professor Fowler smiled and waved. "Izzie, I mean Dorothy, come on down. It appears we're ready to begin."

Izzie dropped her bookbag on the seats and climbed the steps to the stage. She took a deep breath and found her spot, shielding her eyes from the spotlight that must have been flipped around by accident and was pretty much blinding her at the moment. When they finally realized it and moved it out of the way, Scarlett walked up beside with her chin held high, trying her best to accept the fact that she had been cast as the Good Witch—even though the general consensus was that she was playing against her nature.

Professor Fowler started to hum the tune to *Somewhere over the Rainbow*. "All right, Izzie, it's time for you to practice *Somewhere over the Rainbow*. The music will start whenever you're ready."

Izzie was extremely nervous, but since no one seemed to be paying attention to her, talking and laughing amongst themselves as they waited for their cues, she hoped she would breeze right through it without anyone batting an eye. She took a deep breath and pressed her hands against her diaphragm, then glanced at the piano player and nodded. The music started and she closed her eyes, feeling the warmth of the lamps beating down, She pictured herself as Dorothy as she began one of her favorite songs of all time.

"Somewhere over the rainbow
Way up high..."

By the time she finished, everyone had fallen silent and moved to the front rows of the auditorium to listen to her sing. Everyone was shocked by how beautifully she sang. It was as if she had been born to sing that song. Alison sat in the shadows at the back of the auditorium, not wanting to make her friend nervous. She listened to Izzie's beautiful voice flow through the auditorium, but even more beautiful was the soul that sparkled up on the stage. She smiled to herself, proud of how well Izzie was doing.

The door to the left was flung open, startling everyone. The library gnomes, dressed in their Munchkin outfits, ignored the students' snickers and made their way in, walking almost in sync. Behind the Munchkins were several disgruntled freshmen, there to practice their parts as flying monkeys and not really sure how they had been roped into being flying monkeys in the first place. All they remembered was Professor Fowler offering them some sort of cookie, then the next thing they knew they had their flying monkey costumes in hand. It was too late to back out at that point since even the headmistress had thanked them for helping out in the school play. They just hoped that none of their friends showed up.

"I can't believe we got suckered into this," one of the freshmen grumbled to the guy next to him. "This is like the smallest part you could possibly get, and here I am looking ridiculous, with no lines, flapping my arms around the stage like an idiot."

Scarlett giggled and flicked the freshman in the forehead. "Remember, there are no small parts, only small freshmen."

They started another run-through of the entire play.

The cast had already been through it a dozen times, but everyone knew that Professor Fowler wanted absolute perfection. She stood at the front of the stage like a conductor, waving her arms and demanding that people repeat their lines again even if they had gotten them perfect.

Izzie didn't mind, though. She had memorized all her lines, and if this helped the other people in the play, then she was down for it.

Scarlett gritted her teeth and forced a smile. "I can *absolutely* be a happier person. It's what my dreams are about."

"Oh, good," Professor Fowler replied with a chirp, clapping her hands as she walked to the other side of the stage.

Scarlett leaned her head back, rolled her eyes, and shook her fists in irritation. Izzie had to give her some credit. She was trying really hard to sound nice, and for Scarlett, that was a feat in and of itself. She could've just as easily backed out of the play when she didn't get the part she wanted, but instead, she took it and was making the best of it. Izzie had to admit it was kind of strange having a bitchy Good Witch, though.

18

"Here you are, headmistress," one of the students said, handing her the newly-printed issue of the *SNM Times*.

"Thank you, dear," the headmistress replied, taking the paper. She tucked it under her arm as she walked through the hallway shooing the students on to their next class.

When everyone was in the classrooms, the headmistress sat down on a bench and flipped through the newspaper. There were articles about the upcoming finals, a review of the Valentine's Day dance, luckily leaving out the part where the shifters had turned into wolves, and detailing other happenings around the school, including the school play coming soon and the first Louper match of the semester. She smiled and closed the paper, almost missing the article on the front page. However, the picture on the front immediately caught her attention.

Peter had written a piece about the illegal go-kart race that had taken place on school grounds. It was the headline for the new sports section the *Times* had added because of the increased interest in the upcoming Louper matches. She narrowed her eyes and read the article, scoffing at the fact that there weren't any names.

"The speed and fury of this go-kart race were beyond anything I had ever witnessed. The bravery of the racers shone through as they sped through the forest with only three feet of roadway visible before them. If it hadn't been for a blast of dark magic illegally performed by one of the unnamed drivers—you know who you are—a certain sophomore would've been the winner. Unfortunately, the race was broken up directly after that, and the students returned to the school."

Headmistress Berens read the article out loud, her voice growing louder with frustration.

Right at the top of the article was a blurred picture, magically spelled to show the cars racing by too fast to make out any faces. Mara looked up as a student hurried past with her books clutched to her chest, trying not to make eye contact. She cleared her throat and stood up, keeping the frustration out of her voice.

"Melanie, I want you to go fetch Peter for me. You know, the sophomore who…"

Melanie nodded. "I know who Peter is. He works for the newspaper, right?"

Headmistress Berens nodded, and the girl scampered off to find Peter. She sighed and headed to her office to wait for Peter. She tapped her fingers on the newspaper on her desk and looked up at the wooden box on the shelf. As if she didn't have enough to worry about already, now she had to worry about students not only performing illegal acts of magic on school grounds, but the newspaper writing about it.

On top of all of that, she had just dealt with a situation where Izzie had blown a giant hole in the back wall of the potions class, all because she had accidentally inhaled some of the herbs. Now, she was aware that, given the type of herbs that Izzie had inhaled and the manner in which they had been prepared, it could have happened to anyone. The thing that bothered her the most was that Izzie's vision hadn't been sunshine and daisies. It had been violent and dark, just like the past she didn't know she had. The headmistress was now even more concerned that Izzie was starting to remember things that she shouldn't. Even if they came in the form of dreams, memories, or even flashbacks that she wasn't sure were real, it was dangerous. Worst of all, Mara didn't know what to do about it. With the memory orbs collecting dark spots and her inability to locate Izzie's parents, there wasn't a lot she could do. It was too dangerous to tell her the truth, not only for her mind but because of those who were searching for her. It was apparent, though, that the Jasper Elf was becoming far too powerful.

Just then she heard a soft knock on the door.

"Come in," Headmistress Berens called.

"Yes, Headmistress?" Peter asked nervously as he stepped into the office.

"Have a seat." She pushed the newspaper toward him. "I want you to tell me who organized the go-kart race."

Peter took a deep breath and cleared his throat. "I'm sorry, Headmistress, but I can't reveal my sources. It's a rule for reporters."

Headmistress Berens was irritated, there is no doubt about it, but between Peter's response and the serious look on his face she had a hard time resisting a smile. "You know where the line is, right?"

Peter looked confused. "What line?"

"The one where you realize students are in over their heads and can get badly hurt, and it's time to call in reinforcements. You know...before it's too late?"

Peter felt a chill on the back of his neck as he thought about the horrible things that could've happened during that race. Not only because of the opportunity for injury from a crash or an out-of-control go-kart but due to something he hadn't thought about at the time. Not only were there dark family students there, but the school had been plagued by dark magic for two years now. In reality, he wasn't sure whether he'd be quick enough to sense danger and report it before anyone got hurt, and that made him more than slightly nervous.

"I hope so," he said with a shaky voice.

"Me, too. It's a very complex world out there, and some of that world is trying to get in here. As a journalist, you're making a point of keeping an eye on things. I want you to keep in mind that the line is sometimes a lot closer than you think."

The group was starting a brand-new class, something that had been scheduled later in the year since there were many things they needed to learn before they could take it. Professor Rupert Wilson, a Light Elf with silver hair flowing down his back and an air of youth even though he was several hundred years old, was assigned to teach Multi-Dimensional lessons to the sophomores. He was a fun teacher but serious about his work, knowing that it was vital for them to understand that type of magic. It could be beneficial, but at the same time extremely dangerous.

"Greetings! My name is Professor Wilson, and I am your multidimensional class instructor for the semester. You're probably wondering what multidimensional magic is. Well, it's many things, but as far as this class is concerned, it is your opportunity to take a look back through history at some of the most poignant moments and see them not just from one perspective, but from two. If you think about your history texts, you get most of the perspective from the winning side and only a partial view from the losing one. What people don't understand is that it's not always black and white like that. And at the same time, no matter how much we praise the winners, they were not always on the right side."

Professor Wilson picked up a box and began to walk around the classroom, nodding at each student as he handed them a pair of glasses. The students looked at him strangely for a moment, staring at the black-rimmed glasses and wondering why in the world they would need them. All they had expected was a readthrough of a magical text or presentations by special guest speakers, but none of those were in the cards apparently. When all the glasses have been passed out, the professor walked back up to the front and picked up his pair.

"All right, class, go ahead and put on your glasses."

The students put their glasses on and gasped. What looked like a normal pair of glasses was actually not normal at all. When they put them on, they found themselves in a different time and place.

"This is where you will learn how to use everything from all the other classes you have taken so far and combine it to be a great service to yourself and others. In some circumstances, you may even save your own life. First up, the 1968 Chicago riots during the Democratic National Convention, including the clash between the police and the peaceful protesters in Grant Park. I designed it so that the right lens displays the events from the police officers' perspective and the left shows it from the protesters'."

The students watched as thousands of local, state, and federal police officers were sent in to control a few thousand antiwar protesters supporting McCarthy and withdrawal from Vietnam. The professor asked dozens of questions to try to pull things out of them that they hadn't thought of before. While most of them sided with the protesters, they started to understand a little bit better why seeing both sides of the event was important.

"What would you do?"

Kathleen put up her hand. "If I were the protesters, I would've sat down like they did during the Martin Luther King marches. If I were one of the police officers, I would've followed the law and not attacked unarmed people. Some of the cops stood back, but I think standing back is just as bad as running forward if you're not going to do anything to help those that need it."

Ethan shook his head. "I think the cops were in the

wrong, but at the same time, the protesters were taunting them. You have to think about what it's like to stand in front of a group of people being taunted and threatened for hours while doing nothing. Human or magical, we all have the same tolerance levels, and it looks to me like the cops just snapped. That period of time was really volatile, and everyone's emotions were high with the loss of so many lives in Vietnam."

The professor tapped his chin. "If you had been there, how would you have solved it? Would you have used magic? And if you had, what help would that have provided?"

Izzie took a deep breath and raised her hand. "It really depends on the situation. I think that if magic were an everyday thing in human life and the protesters had used it responsibly to calm the situation, it could've helped. At the same time, the cops could've used it to calm the crowd. Unfortunately, most of the crowd wasn't really out of hand, at least not until they were attacked."

They moved through different scenarios, getting caught up in the lesson. Many found themselves switching sides and using an entirely different thought process. Many of them were shocked, reacting in ways they hadn't expected to. By the end of the class, everyone had enjoyed the experience, and they were looking forward to the next one. Some of the students got nauseated from the glasses and were forced to sit with their heads between their knees, taking deep breaths.

Headmistress Berens stopped by the classroom and walked up to the front, chuckling as she passed those trying to control their nausea. Professor Wilson put the last of the glasses back in the box and nodded at the head-mistress. He'd known that she would stop by and had expected her earlier, but he supposed she had been busy with other things. He couldn't even imagine how hard it was to be the headmistress of that school. She leaned against the desk and crossed her arms, nodding at the glasses in the box.

"How did they do?"

Professor Wilson shrugged. "About what you'd expect. There were no real winners, but there was a whole lot of new awareness."

19

It was game day, and the SNM Cardinals were on everyone's lips. The entire school was stoked about the upcoming game. Luke and his teammates nervously paced the floors of the mansion for hours before warm-up began. Even Wyatt and Henry were nervous, and that pretty much never happened.

"It's opening day jitters, that's all." Wyatt rolled his eyes.

"Maybe, or maybe it's the fact that we shouldn't be there, and we're going to lose hard-core," Henry said with panic in his voice.

"You are such a pessimist. You seriously need to relax a little bit. If you walk into the game like this, you're going to be done for within three seconds. You know that nerves get you every single time. I don't know why you do this to yourself."

Wyatt was right, whether Henry wanted to believe it or not. At the first game of the year, he got so nervous that he'd puke before going onto the field. At the same time, the Cardinals had won the first game of the season since he had made the team two years before, so in a way, the jitters were good luck.

That afternoon, the Cardinals' competition was a San Francisco Bay-area private school team, the Sandpipers. Of course, playing this game would be difficult if everyone had to be on location with the other team. If that were the case, they'd end up only playing people from the surrounding area, which for Charlottesville was pretty much no one. Magic allowed the two teams to play from opposite sides of the country without ever setting foot on the same field. It was genius, really. It not only saved the school money, but it saved them from having to break up the inevitable fights that used to happen when they traveled to play each other.

The spectators in the stands could see the teams on both sides of the country, but the players could only see their own team. This allowed the game to stay fair and safe, and be available for just about every high school in the country to play. Wyatt elbowed Henry in the side and nodded at the team.

"They don't look much tougher than they did last year."

Henry chuckled. "Good, because we beat the pants off them last year, and I'd really like to get this over with. I like a challenge. I don't want to end up being bored all the time."

The teams moved to their respective places on the field and lined up. They saw the other team for just long enough to nod and size each other up, then got ready for their own game. Before the teams became invisible to each other, the referee took the center of the field and blew his whistle, putting his hand in the air to gain the attention of the spectators.

"The goal of this game is the same every time," the referee shouted. "From the start, you know exactly where you need to go. In this game, you are going to be moving quietly through Kitengala on the plains, near Kenya, Africa. Whether your team decides to run straight into battle, tag others out for a break, or even send a team to explore the rest of the map, your goal remains the same: find the prize located on your map without dying. Good luck to both teams."

The referee swirled his wand over his head, creating a blue dome over the players. The team across from them disappeared, no longer being projected onto SNM's field. The guys closed their eyes, and when they opened them again, they were standing on the plains of Kenya. The teams would be facing leopards, zombies guarding treasure, the hot sun, and angry local tribes rather than playing tourist. The boys looked at the lush scenery that stretched as far as the eye could see. A herd of gazelles ran in the distance, and a lion crouched next to a nearby bush, stalking its prey.

They had to admit it was absolutely gorgeous, but they knew they weren't there to sightsee. They also knew that lurking in the shadows, and most likely hiding within the buildings of the local town, were the dangers they had to avoid. This was not just some beautiful African plain. It was a virtual world designed to trick them into comfort, then rip them back out and leave them standing on the field feeling like idiots as the people in the stands stared blankly at them. Not one single guy on that team wanted to deal with that.

Wyatt motioned for everyone to gather around. "All right, guys. We know what the goal is. We have an idea of what we're going to be facing, and it's important that we don't get caught up in the scenery. We're playing against another team, and we need to make it to the goal before they do. We work as a team, and when it's down to one person, we cheer them on from the sidelines even if they can't see us. Let's split into three groups. One heads out to the plains, one heads to the town, and one heads down the road toward the animal sanctuary about three miles east of here. You all know what to do if you find the treasure. Trust me, we'll know if you grab it. Good luck out there, guys, and watch each other's backs."

The team put their hands in the center of the circle and shouted their battle cry, as they always did before practice. The nerves were evident on the newbies' faces as they teamed up and started out in their assigned directions. It was unlikely that any of them would see the end of the game from inside the virtual world, but every player had a place in the grand scheme, and every single one of them would play a part, big or small, in getting to the end and finding that treasure.

Luke smeared some black makeup across his cheeks and passed it to his teammates. He was one of the guys heading out to the plains. In his opinion, that was the most likely place to put the treasure because no one wanted to go out there and get eaten by a lion. Most of his teammates were new guys, just like him. The majority of them had never played the game in real mode before. Luke didn't mind, though. He'd only played with his dad, and although he had a natural talent for it, he was quite a bit less sure of himself after the incident at the dance.

"Keep your heads down, boys. There are lots of things out here that would like to take it off your shoulders," Luke whispered as they walked along.

"You okay after the other night?" one of the guys asked.

"I'm fine, but thanks for asking. You're pretty much the only one who has."

"No problem, buddy. I wanted to ask earlier, but I didn't want to put you on the spot in front of everybody. I know how that can be."

Luke patted him on the shoulder and nodded, knowing exactly what he meant. This was the kid who, when he had started out on the team, had barely been able to remember what he was supposed to be doing at any given time. The whole game had been foreign to him. However, as he played with the other guys, he realized it wasn't as bad as he thought. In fact, the kid had gotten pretty good at it, but his big weakness was allowing his mind to drift into tourist mode whenever they had idle time. It was a hard habit to break when you were sent to places you'd never been and had always wanted to go there. Luke was just glad their first virtual game had been on Oriceran. The whole team would've been dead by that point.

Because of what had happened, Luke's confidence had dropped about three notches and with it went his caution. He knelt next to a patch of tall grass without thought, glancing curiously at the other guys when their eyes grew wide and they slowly backed away. He tilted his head to the side, not understanding what they were doing until he heard the crunch of paws behind him. When he twisted his body around, he was face to face with a leopard. Its teeth dripped saliva, and its stomach rumbled loudly enough that Luke shivered. Before he could lift his hands, the leopard attacked. Luke fell back, putting his arm over his face and waiting for the fatal blow.

When he opened his eyes, surprised not to feel the leopard's teeth sinking into him, he realized he had been tagged out early. He was only the fourth guy on the field. He slammed his fist on the ground, humiliated and discouraged. He felt like it was just another thing to add to his misery after what had happened at the dance. On top of that, he'd been avoiding Izzie. Not because he didn't want to see her—he wanted to see her very much—but because he was too embarrassed about what had happened and how he had treated her to face her.

The crowd in the stands were on their feet, cheering loudly for the team. When Luke appeared, though, a deep moan sounded when they realized he was out. They'd all thought he was one of the sure things in this game, but that was the deal with Louper—you never knew when the next bad guy was going to pop around the corner and slice you across the neck. For Luke, it had been a leopard's teeth, but the two other guys in the field got caught in traps set in the dirt. The last one had been eaten by a zombie who was joined by a lion. All of them were first years on the team, so Coach Regency wasn't that surprised. He had hoped for bigger things with Luke, although he was trying to be understanding, knowing what he had just been through.

The game went on and on. Luke took a seat on the side-line bench and watched the game on the big screen. He grimaced every time one of his teammates was tagged. It never failed that they got taken out in the most gruesome and entertaining way possible. It wasn't looking good for them. The other team still had several men on the field and their team was down to Wyatt, who seemed to be lost at the moment. Wyatt fought valiantly though, and in the end, to everyone's surprise, the Cardinals won.

The fans had sat there stunned as Wyatt wandered into a small cave at the edge of the plain and found himself in front of the trophy before any of the Sandpipers. It wasn't just brawn that had won them the game. It was brains too, and a whole hell of a lot of luck. The prize was coins that would be split up among them equally to spend in the kemana, On top of that, they found themselves one step closer to getting into the championship tournament, something Luke was hoping they would make it to even though this was his first year.

Luke, wanting to be a good sport, walked over to Wyatt and shook his hand. "You did a badass job, dude. I'm sorry I went out so early."

Wyatt chuckled and shrugged. "Just so you know, in my first game one of the nomad soldiers sliced my head off my shoulders as soon as I entered the world. I didn't even get to see the map."

They both laughed. Luke was just happy that for once Wyatt wasn't giving him a hard time.

20

Alison, Izzie, Kathleen, Emma, Aya, and Peter sat in the front row of the stadium waving their SNM flags and cheered for both Luke and Ethan. To their surprise, Luke was tagged out before Ethan. From what they could see, Ethan had found a pretty good hiding space jutting out from behind a rundown shanty in the village. He stabbed zombies in the throat while the other guys searched for the treasure. He actually ended up making it longer than any of the first years, but finally found his doom when a tribe member speared him in the back.

"Great." Kathleen rolled her eyes and sighed. "Now we get to hear Ethan's big head go on about how he made it longer than any of the first years. I knew this would be a disaster when he joined the team."

Emma laughed. "Is it a disaster for you or for him?"

Kathleen shrugged her shoulders. "I don't know, but either of them is terrible. I really don't want it to be me, but I have a feeling it'll end up on my shoulders."

The girls and Peter cheered on the rest of the team, even though the guys they had come to see were on the bench. When Wyatt appeared with the gold in his hands, the whole stadium roared in excitement. The stomping of their feet on the bleachers and their cheers drifted over the hills and through the valleys of Charlottesville, Virginia.

"Hey," Alison said softly after a glance at Izzie's energy, "don't be so sullen. We won!"

"I'm trying." Izzie sighed and shook her head. "I just wish I could get Luke's attention. He's so caught up in the sports stuff that there's suddenly no room for me."

"It won't always be like this. Eventually, people lose interest."

"Hopefully, for Luke's sake, they don't. He really likes feeling like he's part of something instead of being some shifter that people make fun of but are really afraid of."

"Hey, I have an idea! Want to come with the rest of us to the mall? We're all going to go over there after the game. We'll get some lunch, do some shopping, probably carry some of Kathleen's enormous number of bags around..." Izzie laughed, knowing exactly how that would be. She had been shopping with Kathleen far too many times.

Alison squeezed Izzie's hand, giving her a pouty face. "Please, please! Do it for me, and do it so Luke can just let go and have some fun with his team in the kemana. I promise he won't forget you while he's down there. Some space for both of you isn't a bad thing, You know now that Luke has friends you can trust him around, and they won't turn their backs on him."

Izzie giggled and rolled her eyes, squeezing Alison's hand back. "Of course, I'll go with you. And you know what, you're probably right. This a big deal for the team, and I don't want to distract him from that."

The whole group got up and waited for the team to clear the field, Luke waving at Izzie before he disappeared with the others. She sighed and shrugged, then jogged to catch up with her school family so they could head into town and have a good time. They grabbed the jitney from the gate and rode it into town, getting off just a few blocks from the Charlottesville open-air shopping location that they called the mall.

The day started out great. They meandered into the various stores, window-shopped, and watched Kathleen buy everything her heart desired. They talked about how they missed the guys—all except Peter and Tanner, of course, since they were with them. Tanner had become a part of the family. Ethan and Luke, though, were staples in the group, and even Kathleen was a little bit bummed that she didn't have somebody to mess with now that Ethan was on the Louper team. Still, they did their best to have a good time and enjoy their weekend out and about with all the normals.

"What's up with that group of normals over there?" Kathleen asked, glancing at a group of a dozen or so non-magicals standing next to one of the shops. They snuck glares at the girls and Peter and Tanner.

Tanner stepped forward with his shoulders back, feeling as if he should be the protector. He did not understand what kind of magic Izzie and Alison had. "Maybe we should just go the other way. It's obvious they don't want us here."

Emma tilted her head to the side and stared at them. "Do you think they know we're magicals?"

Aya shook her head. "I seriously doubt it. But we all have to admit we're a little bit different than the normals around here, so it doesn't surprise me that they're staring us down. I just hope they leave us alone."

The others nodded and started past the group. They'd only made it about halfway when the normals surrounded them, poking fun at their age, their clothes, and the school insignia on their backpacks. "You're from that pathetic little school over the hill, huh? The one they say people do magic in."

The normals laughed, thinking that was absolutely ludicrous. Tanner, Peter, Emma, Izzie, and the others stayed in a tight circle. Alison stared at their souls and found that none of them had dark magic in them. Rather, they were the way they were because they had *no* magic in them. She couldn't imagine how they would be if they knew she could do magic.

Tanner stepped up to the main guy and stared him right in the eyes while puffing out his chest. "We didn't do anything to you guys. We're just trying to have a good day off. Go pick on somebody else."

The normal flipped the toothpick around in his mouth and smirked, staring Tanner up and down. "Well, look who it is. The watchdog finally stepped up."

Tanner just looked at him, unsure if he knew the truth or if that was just a normal's figure of speech. Either way, Tanner decided to ignore it. He rolled his eyes, flicked his hand at the guy, and turned away. That apparently was not the right thing to do. The normal grabbed him by the arm and pushed him into his friends. The townies got a little more aggressive with every passing moment. Alison, Izzie, and the others started to wonder if they were going to have to use their magic.

Using magic in public was strictly forbidden, and none of them really wanted to get in any more trouble than they had already been in that year. Izzie clapped her hands to get their attention.

"Hey, you guys need to just get the hell out of here and leave us alone. We didn't do anything to you, and we don't have anything for you."

"And not only will you have to deal with these guys, which I promise you don't want to, but you're also gonna have to deal with us too," a voice called from behind them.

Everyone turned quickly, smiling as they saw the group of kids they had met the semester before. Their faces were stony, and they were ready for a fight. Izzie and the others had to admit it that it was the first time they had been ecstatic to see a group of humans. When they had started their integration classes, no one had been excited about it. It was just more time spent doing what they'd been doing their entire lives: hiding from the public, hiding their magic, and pretty much hiding who they were. But when they met the group of kids at the luncheon and then later on the field trip, they had started to make friends, friends who understood their secret and had yet to reveal it to anyone.

"Oh, fantastic." The leader of the townies chuckled. "Now we have to deal with the idiots from the prep school.

I thought you guys were rivals? Whatever. We'll just catch you guys next time."

The group watched as the townies walked away snickering at the magicals, not understanding who they had come across. When they were out of sight, Izzie and the others turned back toward the humans, more than grateful for what they had done for them. Peter leaned toward Alison and grabbed her hand, squeezing it tightly.

"Integration actually works!" Peter whispered, making Alison giggle.

"Thanks a lot, guys," Tanner said, shaking each of the guys' hands. He hadn't met them the year before, but he was always up for making friends, human or not.

"It's no problem," the largest of the kids said pulling his bookbag onto his shoulder. "Your friend Ethan pretty much saved my life that day at the restaurant. If I would've gotten expelled, my parents would never have let me live it down. Besides, we like you guys. You're no different from the kids we go to school with, except that you're pretty cool people."

None of them expected humans to be nice to them, even if they didn't know who they were. But this group of kids, after only hanging out with them twice, had put their butts on the line for them. Emma whispered something in Kathleen's ear, and she smiled at her.

"I think it's a perfect idea." She looked at the normals. "You guys want to spend a few hours with us here in the mall? We're just hanging out and not really doing anything, but it would give us all a chance to get to know each other without the teachers breathing down our necks and wondering if we're telling you all of our magical secrets."

Everybody chuckled, and the normals nodded. Two of them were still dressed in their school uniforms. It seemed the prep school was a little bit harder on those kids than the School of Necessary Magic was on their students. Alison, Izzie and the others were relieved to spend a few hours with the normals. It held the stares to a minimum and kept that other group away from them, even though they lurked around the area and turned up every place the group did.

Izzie knew they were all a bit strange, but she didn't think it was noticeable enough for the humans to pick on them. It was the first time she'd experienced bullies she didn't know and she wondered if it was like that for all humans. Of course, bullying was bullying no matter where you went to high school, and the School of Necessary Magic was no exception. The upperclassmen bullied the lower classmen, the people in the classes bullied each other, the jocks bullied the non-jocks, the intellectuals bullied the non-intellectuals, and so forth, making bullying just as bad in the magical community as it was in the human one. The only advantage the normals had was that when they inflicted their bullying on the magical community, the magicals had to find non-magical ways to deal with it.

Alison and Tanner walked hand in hand at the back of the group, talking about the different things that had happened that day and laughed about the moment when Ethan had been stabbed in the back. Of course, had he really been hurt they wouldn't be laughing, but he was fine, which allowed them to make fun of him for pretty much anything he did on the field. He was shopping in the kemana with his team at that moment. Little did he know he'd be tortured by Kathleen and the rest when he got back for making such a big mistake.

It was the will and the way for the group of eight, a group that referred to themselves as a family.

21

The year rolled by. Before they knew it, the birds were chirping loudly outside the windows, the skies were a beautiful blue, and the temperatures were a comfortable sixty-five degrees day and night. It was almost everybody's favorite time of the year. The students emerged from the ice-covered cocoon of winter, excited to see nature growing and blooming to create a beautiful landscape around the mansion.

Izzie and Alison leaned against the picnic tables in the courtyard, just taking in the fresh air. Izzie couldn't believe how alive everything was. The crocuses had started to push through the ground, and the daffodils swayed in the cool spring air. Alison leaned her head back and closed her eyes, feeling the warmth of the sun cascading over her skin. While she loved the winter wonderland at the school, spring had always been her favorite. The energies were alive around her, and people's souls had happy wisps of wild colors flowing through them as they walked through the courtyard to different classes or different events.

Kathleen, Emma, Aya, Luke, and Tanner followed Peter and Ethan through the foyer, laughing as Ethan teased Peter with hints about what his prank for that year's April Fool's Day would be. Suffice it to say, very few people were planning to eat lunch in the cafeteria that day. Those who were wanted to find out what prank Ethan had in mind, even if it meant they were the butt of the joke.

"Not only did I decide not to eat lunch in the cafeteria, I also decided to stay as far away from you as I possibly can," Kathleen informed the prankster, shaking her head. "I don't care how epic your joke was last year. I still think April Fool's Day is stupid."

Ethan looked over his shoulder at Kathleen and winked. "If you think last year's was epic, you haven't seen anything yet. Just wait for this year's. It will blow everyone away."

Peter pointed his finger at Ethan. "Is that a hint? Are you doing something with explosives?"

Ethan laughed and shook his head. "I'm not going to tell you what I'm doing. All I'm going to tell you is that it will be epic. Well, I guess I should say it's not explosive in the way that you're thinking, Peter. I hate to break it to you, but not everyone bursts into flames every time they try a magic spell."

They headed over to Izzie and Alison, laughing at Peter's sulking. Emma patted him on the shoulder, and he blushed and let out a deep breath. He watched as everyone else started to make their way back into the mansion, headed toward the gym for the day's big event.

"Are you ready to go, guys?" Ethan said clapping his hands and rubbing them together.

Emma lifted her eyebrows and looked at Kathleen. "The real question is, are you ready to go, Kathleen?"

Kathleen scoffed and shrugged. "Please! I can debate these idiots into the ground in my sleep."

Although Kathleen looked calm and cool on the outside, Alison knew better. She saw the wild colors of nerves flowing through Kathleen's energy and twisting where her chest would be. Alison felt bad for her, but she knew it would only embarrass her further if she brought it up. Instead, she stood up and put her arm around Kathleen's shoulder.

"Let's get this show on the road."

The group made their way into the gym, where the Future Leaders Club was sponsoring the speeches of the three students from each class who were running for class president for the next year. They'd also set up a debate between the three juniors who were campaigning for student body president. When they entered the gym, Kathleen veered off, flipping through her note cards as she made her way to the stage.

"Come on, Kathleen, get it together. There's no reason to be nervous," Kathleen whispered to herself as she climbed the stairs.

In reality, Kathleen was terrified, and even down in the seats of the auditorium, Alison could see that swirling around in her energy.

She leaned over and whispered to Izzie, "Kathleen may be playing it cool for us, but I can tell she's more nervous than she's ever been before. You think maybe there's something you could do for her?" Alison wiggled her eyebrows at Izzie, who burst into laughter.

"I think I can work something out," Izzie replied, rubbing her hands together.

Izzie decided to use some of her newly-discovered power to help her dear friend Kathleen. She took a deep breath and held her hands palms-up as the magic flowed through her, making her skin glow just slightly as symbols flipped up and down her arms and across her neck. She released a current of calming energy that floated over the crowd and up onto the stage, seeping over to Kathleen's feet and sinking into her skin before she realized it.

Professor Powell, who was standing to the side, monitored the students as they took their seats to make sure no one caused any problems. He saw the symbols out of the corner of his eye and studied Izzie. He snapped his head to the side when he heard the headmistress on the stage, but she had missed what had happened. He glanced at Kathleen, who was now a little calmer. She'd managed to take a deep breath and let it out, slowly relaxing as she stood first in line to give her speech.

"Welcome, students, to the political presentations and debates sponsored by the Future Leaders Club," Headmistress Berens said, and she clapped her hands, forcing the rest of the auditorium to follow along. "For our first presentation, we will be hearing from Kathleen, who is running for junior class president next year. Please put your hands together and give her a warm welcome."

All the students clapped, and Ethan, Emma, and Aya stood up and whistled loudly, making as much noise as they could until Kathleen was behind the podium. Izzie squeezed Alison's hand, able to tell that her spell had worked. Kathleen was back to her normal calm and collected self, tapping her cards on the podium and standing tall and proud.

"I want to start the speech today by saying I really appreciate anyone who has thought about or decided to vote for me for junior class president. I can tell you right now it would be a great honor to represent you during our junior year in high school. It is a year of preparation, a year of excitement, and a year to make memories leading up to our final days here. That said, one thing I've learned since coming to the school is that things aren't always as they seem. I've had to step out of my bubble, and I've started to understand how to grow beyond the idea of us versus them. There've been more times than I can count over the last two years where people have shocked me by being there for me when I never thought I would even speak to them. My best friends are a group of ragtag misfits who are sometimes put down by others, but that never puts out their flame or makes them angry or bitter. All it does is make them more motivated to be there for others who are in similar positions to theirs. When it all comes down to it, it's not about who's right or wrong. That idea is in the eye of the beholder. We are all different, we all think differently, we all act differently, and we all want different things. I want us to work together to make everyone's dreams come true. If I am elected as your junior class president, I will make sure we make the magical world even more beautiful than it already is for the future. Thank you for listening, and please vote for me for junior class president."

Everyone clapped again, and three-quarters of the students were on their feet, whistling loudly. Kathleen laughed and curtsied before she made her way off the stage. The rest of the candidates got up and made their speeches. One focused on field trips, the ability to go to the kemana anytime they wanted, and the creation of a student organization that would help the professors track down dark magic that happened on the school grounds. He was one of the students who had wanted to do more when the boy had been struck down by a curse the previous year. The last of the junior class president candidates was all about saving the Earth, keeping their grounds safe and beautiful, and implementing anything that had to do with reusing, recycling, and environmental friendliness.

When they were done, Headmistress Berens took the stage again. "Thank you, you three, for those wonderful speeches," she said, clapping her hands. "Now we are going to hear from the three candidates for student body president: Wyatt, Scarlett, and Farrell."

As soon as Farrell's name was mentioned someone in the audience howled, and the headmistress spun, narrowing her eyes and pointing her finger at the miscreant. Scarlett went first, giving a rousing speech about togetherness, and helping her fellow man. When she was done, her cronies and half of the people who were afraid of her gave her a standing ovation, while others looked down at the floor. Scarlett played nice and kept a sweet smile on her face the entire time, even though everyone knew she was taking names and wouldn't forget. Next was Wyatt's short speech, then Farrell's. Both got through them pretty quickly so they could start the debate.

The Future Leaders Club president took the podium and turned to the three candidates, clearing his throat.

"The debate will be about the place of magic in today's society, and whether we should be increasing the amount of magic we present to the normals to prepare them for the opening of the Oriceran gates thousands of years from now."

Each candidate gave their opinion, and most were similar. When it was Farrell's turn he started to speak, but then suddenly stopped and watched a magical surge of energy shaped like a wolf, shoot down the aisle, which then flowed through his body. Normally, that would be considered just a fun practical joke played on a shifter, but with everything going on it didn't seem as innocent as it should have. Most people thought it had been Scarlett, but when Alison glanced at Scarlett's soul, she didn't believe she was responsible. Someone was messing with the elections, and a magical running shifter was only the beginning.

March was over before they knew it, and the group found themselves waking up on a beautiful spring morning that just happened to be April Fool's Day. Everyone crept through their dorms slowly, keeping their eyes peeled for anything that might have to do with Ethan's practical joke. No one wanted to catch the brunt of it, but they also couldn't spend their entire day looking over their shoulders. Izzie and Alison stayed behind to finish getting ready while the others made their way down to get breakfast in the cafeteria. Each person crept through the doors of the cafeteria, paused to check if they'd been enchanted, and let out a deep sigh of relief.

"I don't know what he has planned, but whatever it is, we're probably all going to regret coming out of our rooms today," Alison whispered, making Izzie giggle as they made their way downstairs.

They sat around their normal table eating whatever they chose for breakfast. Ethan was suspiciously absent from his seat. No one wanted to ask where he was, because they all knew he would eventually appear. When the first bell rang and all the food disappeared from their plates, they felt relieved that they had at least made it through breakfast without any crazy practical jokes being played on them. As the students started to file out of the cafeteria, no one was really paying attention to the people in front of them, and students began to disappear.

Alison and Izzie were talking about the upcoming Louper game and the play that was just around the corner. When they stepped over the threshold of the cafeteria, they screamed. Their feet never hit the floor, and they were bombarded by the sensation of falling fast. Izzie looked around her, but nothing but white light surrounded the girls. Alison clutched Izzie tightly, seeing the energy whirling around her. They finally began to slow down, and their feet gently landed on the ground. Birds twittered around them. When the light dissipated, they found themselves standing with a large group of schoolmates about three miles from the mansion near the edge of the orchards.

"That little weasel," Kathleen ground out, narrowing her eyes. "We are all going to be late to class, and we're going to be dirty from trudging through the mud. He's going to be the only one there on time, while the professors wonder where the heck we are."

Izzie laughed loudly. "Wouldn't that be the best April Fool's Day joke ever? Not that he dropped us out here, but that he was actually on time for class for once in his life."

22

It might have been all fun and games on April Fool's Day at the School of Necessary Magic, but when the sun dipped below into the horizon, the crickets started to chirp, and the clouds drifted across the moon to darken the streets of Charlottesville, dark magic started seeping in slowly. The magical who lived in the town had become accustomed to the feeling of dark magic, especially with the students who were now permitted to attend the school and their parents who traveled back and forth checking on their children or dropping them off after the breaks. So, when a couple of dark wizards decided to meet in an empty building just off the Charlottesville Cemetery, no one flinched at the dark energy floating around them.

"You know what I think? I think it's hilarious that they put up all these traps and sensors to make sure that we didn't get back into town, and then what do they do? Allow the dark families to send their kids to the school. I don't know why they wouldn't think we would take total advantage of that."

The older dark wizard smiled, adjusting the hood of his robe as he sat on the stone sarcophagus inside the building. His long gray hair cascaded out from underneath the hood and covered some of the wrinkles that creased his cheeks and forehead. He was a powerful wizard who had practiced dark magic for many centuries, including those spent with Rhazdon on Oriceran.

"I told you, these light beings put too much faith in the obvious. They think that they can fool us, chase us away, and even keep us out." The wizards laughed loudly, and their voices echoed off the wood planks of the old shack that held cracked and broken tombstones and other graveyard accoutrements, yard equipment, and a small desk for the cemetery's groundskeeper.

"They have tried to keep us out for centuries, Phaedrus. But with your enormous powers, you know better than anyone that there is no way they can keep us out forever. We always find a way." The younger wizard removed his hood, letting his dark hair stream down the back of his gown.

Phaedrus nodded and twirled his wand through his fingers like a baton. "Young Apollo." He smiled at the other wizard. "You're much wiser than I thought you would be. But what really gets me is that right now we don't have access to the young minds we need to manipulate. The youth are the power behind all the dark and light magic. Sure, the elders like me are there to push them in the right direction, teach them, and clean up the mess if it gets too bad, but they are the true players. We need them in order to move forward."

Apollo bit his lip and paced back and forth in the small

space with his hands clasped behind him. They'd come to Charlottesville for a purpose, just as they had come there right after Headmistress Berens had taken care of the three dark wizards and their secret hiding place. They had tried to clean up the mess quickly, but it was too late. The school was already on the alert, looking for any trace of dark magic in the streets, in the school, or anywhere near the school grounds. They had made it almost impossible for the dark families and those wizards still looking to complete their mission to have any idea what was happening within the school.

Apollo nodded and took a deep breath, stopping in front of Phaedrus. "Unfortunately, our plan for the toombie failed, leaving a boy only partially injured and able to be restored by the professors at the school. Meanwhile, they figured out exactly what we were up to, and they're expecting us to follow through with that."

"Which means it's time for a new plan." Phaedrus smiled evilly.

"It's getting difficult to make plans when we have dark families sending their children to the school," Apollo replied, rolling his eyes. "What do they think will happen, that the light magic beings will erase the darkness from their souls? That's not how it works. And they're getting in the way of what we need to do."

"Take a deep breath, Apollo. All is not lost. It doesn't really matter that some of these families and others from around the country have sent their kids to the school. In fact, I think it will play along perfectly with one specific plan I've been thinking hard about lately."

Apollo leaned back on a stack of chairs and listened

excitedly as his mentor explained a plan he had been trying to put together since long before the toombie thing came about. "You see, Apollo, we can use these children to make a statement, not only to the light magic, but to the dark families that seem to have forgotten where they came from. It all starts out with a scare, don't you understand that? We can't just threaten these families. They have just as much power as some of us do. We can put their children in danger, which will create a war. These plans don't have to be dramatic or drawn out. Some of the simplest plans in history have turned into some of the greatest victories this world has ever seen. Just think, a group of soldiers at war with another group built a large horse, hid within it, and were welcomed inside their enemies' gates, only to slaughter all their people. Something simple can be used on magical people as well. We have just as many naïve witches and wizards and elves as light magicals do."

Apollo chuckled and rubbed his hands together excitedly. "What should we start with, then? Do we release a couple of nasty-looking creatures to break through the school's glamours? They could really tear up some of that property, including some of the vicious little professors who think they can beat out the dark families. I especially would love to see Headmistress Berens' head waving high above the mansion's roof on a stick."

Phaedrus chuckled and slapped Apollo on the back, shaking his head. "I like how motivated you are. I like that you think outside the box, but I'm going to need you to reel it in just a little bit and think about the repercussions of any actions you take. Releasing creatures like that on the school grounds would be a little bit too harsh. There would be no question in anyone's mind, including the professors, the school, and the government, that we were behind that. We don't want to jump in headfirst and expose ourselves in one fell swoop. We need to make the humans scared, but in a way that doesn't expose too much of where it's coming from."

Phaedrus walked over to the window and looked out across the cemetery grounds, scraping his nail against the glass to cut through the mist that had settled on it. He liked the passion Apollo displayed when he brought him in on this, but at some point, he was afraid that he would be too overzealous for his own good. If Phaedrus didn't rein him in, he could very well give them all away without even knowing it.

"My original idea was along the line of the monsters, but now that I'm here, I understand that that is too much and too strong. We need something that is strong enough to make them notice, but not so strong that they run. It is better to lull them into complacency than force them by overly harsh actions. There is a time and a place for force, but because of their powers—and to avoid a bloody battle yet again between the dark families and the lights—we need to approach this gently."

Apollo nodded and joined Phaedrus at the window. "We need something else, but what that is I have no idea."

Suddenly the door to the building squeaked open. Standing in the doorway, cloaked in shadows, was a dark figure. The two dark wizards drew their wands, but the man stepped forward, put up his hand, and shook his head before closing the door behind him. He pulled his hood down, revealing his dark black hair and full peppered beard. He had a scar that ran from the corner of his eye down his cheek and to the edge of his mouth.

"I have a way," the shadowy man announced. "I've already even road-tested it for you. All you would need to do is follow my instructions, and before you know it, you'll have them lulled into submission and eating out of your hand."

Phaedrus stepped forward, narrowing his eyes. "Who are you?"

The man shook his head. "A friend. Someone who has the same interests as you. Someone who has already started the battle, and can tell you exactly what will happen as you carry out the plan. I stood by and watched the failure of the toombie, but I knew from the beginning that it would never work. Light magic is getting stronger, and there are those out there who can control both it and dark magic at the same time."

"You're talking about the girl. She's been dead for a while now."

The shadowy man didn't say a word, just stroked his beard and waited for the wizards to decide whether they wanted his help. Phaedrus spotted the mark of the dark families and realized that whether he was from their family or not, he was on their side. Phaedrus patted Apollo on the shoulder and nodded, letting him know that everything would be all right.

"All right, stranger with the mark of the dark families, what is your plan?"

The shadowy man smirked. "It's a trick we played—

something you may have seen two decades ago when one of the most recent battles between the light and the dark families resonated through the air. It's actually quite simple. You poison the shifters, so they can't control when they turn from their human form to their wolf. You don't just do it nonchalantly as they did in the past, turning one shifter in the middle of the big city. You need to turn multiple shifters at one time, and you do it during some sort of event where the students are gathered since that will have the most impact. You can't do it at night slithering through the shadows, you have to do it in broad daylight when no one expects to see a shifter in full wolf form. For some reason, it makes much more of an impact to see that change in the daytime than it does to watch those amber eyes disappear into the woods. You have a few wolves running around their precious children, and I can promise you not only will the dark families pick up and run, but so will the light ones. It will just keep rolling from there. Fingers will be pointed, allegations will be made, and the war will be reborn. It will leave the school wounded and incapable of fully protecting itself. What you seek will find you when it has no other choice but to do so."

Phaedrus leaned against the desk, staring at the man as he talked. When he finished, silence fell over the hut. Apollo looked at the men, unsure what Phaedrus would say. They had used that weapon in the past, although not in that way. Not until recently had they started to focus on the children, finding that not only did they hold the power that the dark wizards needed, but they were also excellent bargaining chips. You could draw a powerful light wizard, witch or elf out of anywhere, even the villages of Oriceran, if they thought that their child was in danger.

Phaedrus slowly nodded and a small chuckle built in his chest, expanding into a full-blown deep laugh. Apollo laughed as well, realizing that they had just made a decision. They would attack the shifters, and in doing so, they would be attacking the school as a whole.

23

It was game day again, and the weather wasn't quite as beautiful in Charlottesville as it had recently been. The skies overhead were gray and cloudy. Sprinkles of rain came down over the students as they stood in the stands supporting their team, donning their SNM raincoats and galoshes. As usual, Alison, Tanner, Izzie, Kathleen, Emma, Aya, and Peter took the front row of the stands, rooting for Luke and Ethan as they faced the Philadelphia Coyotes. The teams lined up on the field to listen to the ref as he reviewed the rules, then misted the magic over them.

When they opened their eyes, they found themselves on the beautiful island of Kauai, the oldest of the Hawaiian Islands. Their game boots sank into the white-sand beaches as the crystal-clear blue waters splashed against the shore to their left. Looming mountains covered in lush green forests rose to their right. The boys took a deep breath remembering that they couldn't get caught up in the scenery regardless of the beautiful natural waterfalls, hidden caves, picturesque mountains, and lush forests.

They were playing the Coyotes, and they had to keep their heads in the game.

"Like the rest of you, I'd like to just lie down right here and take a vacation," Wyatt joked. "But we all need to remember what we're here to accomplish. We are one step closer to the championship. Every team we beat, the closer our school gets to taking home the trophy. Let's keep our heads in our game, look out for any threats, and watch each other's backs the entire way."

The boys all nodded and clapped their hands, pumped up for the game. They knew that beyond the beautiful landscape around them, darkness was hiding and waiting to take them out. Sometimes it was in the form of a person or creature, and sometimes it was the actual beauty that got you tagged out of the game. For that reason, they couldn't trust anything they saw, not even the sand beneath their feet or the bright sun in the sky above them. Luke stood next to Wyatt, nodding and rubbed his hands together. Ethan was across the group from them, ready for battle. Ready to do what he was best at: taking out the enemy as quickly as he could before they took him out.

Henry cleared his throat and rolled his shoulders, then looked at his teammates. "The Coyotes are known to play dirty. Last year, they cheated every chance they got."

Ethan chuckled and nodded. "They have the right team name, then."

Henry nodded. "That they do, so watch out for them just as much as the other things in this game. Luke, you and your team head up the mountain. Wyatt, you and your team head along the beach, and I'll take my team through the forest. Remember, there are chests out there, there are hints, and there are special weapons that we can use to win this game. Do your best, guys. Our trophy is waiting for us."

The guys brought their hands together in the center as they always did. This time they quietly gave the battle cry, not wanting to give away their location. The three groups took off in their assigned directions. Henry and his group snuck slowly into the forest and paused to listen for any sound other than the birds chirping in the trees above them. As they crept through, Henry took a right to scope out the clearing he could see ahead. There was a chest in the center of it, which he knew they needed to retrieve it as quickly as possible. If the other team got there first, the chest would disappear and they'd be left wondering what had been inside it.

As Henry crept ahead, he heard a crunch of leaves. He froze and looked around for a moment, then continued forward. As he took the next step, one of the Coyotes grabbed him from behind, covered his mouth, and dragged him into a small cave behind them, where he tagged him out of the game. The others, unaware that Henry had been taken, continued forward and were ambushed when they reached the edge of the clearing. Several Coyote players dashed in, knocking the Cardinals down and injuring them both in the game and in real life.

Out in the stands, Izzie slammed her hands on the railing, shaking her head and pointing. "The Coyotes aren't even supposed to be able to see them. They're cheaters."

Inside the game, all hell had broken loose. The Coyotes snuck into the Cardinals' playing field and chased them all throughout their map. Every time a Cardinal had a chance, a Coyote pushed him off the cliff or stopped him with whatever weapon they could find, tagging him out of the game. The Cardinals tried to stay hidden, but the Coyotes struck when they least expected it. It was a free-for-all inside, and the Cardinals were at a loss for what to do.

Wyatt and the others had caught wind of what was going on and headed into the dark forest. They chased down any advantage to unlock secrets. They jumped over fallen trees and slid beneath ones that tried to crush them. They dodged arrows and boulders, but the Coyotes took them down one at a time. The Coyotes' strategy was working. One by one, the Cardinals popped up in the field, unable to see the map any longer. Some of them were slightly injured, and others needed serious medical attention. This game was not the same as others, which motivated the boys even further to push harder.

Wyatt grabbed Luke by the collar and pulled him close while shaking his head. "They're in here. I don't know how they did it, but they're in here. They are taking us down one at a time. We have to get to the chests first. If we don't get those advantages, we're never going to find the trophy and win this thing. I think we're the only ones left. You go right, I'll go left, and we'll meet in the center of the island."

Luke nodded and pounded Wyatt's fists, then bolted to the right as fast as he could, dodging anything that came in his direction. He could see a light ahead of him that he thought might be a clearing, but as he reached the edge of the woods, he realized it was a cliff. He windmilled his arms to try to slow down and skidded to a stop right at the edge of the cliff. He clutched his chest and breathed heavily, chuckling. As he turned around to continue toward the center of the island, he froze. A Coyote a foot taller than him stared down at him with a smirk on his face. Luke put his hands up and shook his head.

"You aren't supposed to be here."

"But we are…"

The Coyote grabbed Luke by the collar, walked him backward, and dangled him over the edge. His opponent started to laugh and dropped Luke to the rocks below. Luke opened his eyes breathing heavily, looked around the field, and realized he'd been tagged out of the game. He ran over to the coach and shook his head.

"They are cheating. They took over our map, and they've killed every single one of our guys except for Wyatt. I don't see how he can stand up to them on his own."

Coach Regency was watching the game just like the people in the stands. Wyatt ran to the center of the island and stood staring at the trophy. There didn't seem to be anyone else around, but he walked carefully, flexing his hand, ready to lunge for the trophy. Luke couldn't see what was going on, but the spectators screamed at Wyatt to watch out behind him. Coach Regency grimaced as the edge of a boulder smacked Wyatt in the back of the head.

Wyatt woke up in the field, clenching his fists and grinding his teeth. The whole team had been kicked out, and the Coyotes had won. That not only meant they lost the trophy, but they'd were out of contention in the tournament as well. It was a travesty and everyone knew it, including the crowd, who were on their feet chanting, "Cheaters, cheaters!" They saw what had happened and demanded fair play, but the game continued, showing the

Coyotes in their virtual field scanning the grounds as the Coyote players disappeared. Their spell wore off when they grabbed the trophy.

Alison, Izzie, and the rest of them stood with the rain pouring down over their heads and running down their faces. The whole stadium was silent, the only sound the rain as it pattered on the metal bleachers. The Cardinals dropped their gear and lined up in the center of the field with their heads down and their hands clenched, too angry to face their fans. For several moments it was complete silence, then, out of nowhere, one person began to clap. Another person joined in, then another, and then another until everyone in the stands roared loudly in recognition of the champions in front of them. They might not have gotten the trophy or continued to the tournament championship, but they had battled valiantly. They'd been defeated, not by skill or strength, but by cheating, which the Cardinals would never have stooped to even to win a trophy.

Headmistress Berens clapped her hands as she made her way down onto the field. She walked in front of each and every one of the players on the Cardinals Louper team and shook their hands, letting them know they had done a fantastic job. The crowd cheered as each of the players lifted his head, realizing they had nothing to be ashamed of. The headmistress walked to the center of the field, pressed her glowing hand to her throat, and allowed her voice to echo through the stadium.

"The Cardinals, in my opinion, played better than any team I've ever seen play in any of the high schools as long as I have been the headmistress of the school. They might not stand on the field of champions or receive a fancy little trophy with their names engraved on it, but today they showed not only us but everyone watching, including the Coyotes, that we are a school with moral strength and values. We will not stoop to what is wrong. We will not allow the negative and dark to enter the school under any circumstances. I couldn't be prouder of these boys, and I think that deserves a little bit of a treat."

The headmistress smiled as everyone cheered, and grabbed the coach's assistant. "Go tell the kitchen staff we're going to have an ice cream bar—enough to feed the entire school. We are celebrating the Cardinals for playing by the rules even when it wasn't easy."

24

The celebration went on until late in the evening, and everyone went to bed in a positive mood. That was really important to the headmistress. She wanted to show that even through adversity, even when the darkest times hit them, they were able to bounce back and see the light in everything around them. Even the dark kids had a good time, glad that they'd risen above what the Coyotes had done to their Louper team. Everyone was exhausted after being drenched in the rain, having an ice cream social, and laughing way past curfew.

When the girls got upstairs, they took showers and got ready for bed. It wasn't long after they'd laid down that Kathleen, Emma, and Aya were fast asleep in their beds, curled up under the blankets and dreaming of Louper championships and beating the crap out of the Coyotes the next time they saw them. Izzie and Alison, however, were in their normal routine. Izzie couldn't sleep because of her dreams, and Alison had already meditated twice that day, so she was wide awake.

"Come on," Izzie said giddily as she climbed out of bed. "Let's go for a walk. It's a beautiful night."

Alison scanned Izzie's energy. It was the first time she had seen her positive for several days. "Absolutely! What else did you think we would do with our night?"

The girls held back the giggles as they pulled on their galoshes and hung their raincoats over their arms, hoping the rain would have stopped by the time they got out there. They crept through the dorm room to the hall, and down the steps to the front doors. No one was up. Everyone was too exhausted, and even the teachers were tucked into their cottages.

Izzie looked at the sky as they walked across the lawn. "The rain has stopped."

"I can't see it, but I sure don't feel it." Alison giggled.

The air was warm even though it was nighttime, and that early warm spell had all the flowers in bloom around them. Even in the dark, Izzie could see the bright colors of the flowers in the meadows, and Alison smelled their sweet scent as they walked carefully around them and down the hill toward the secluded part of the forest. They didn't have many more nights when they would get to walk outside together since summer was coming. They would head off in their own directions, doing their own things and waiting for the day they got back together when school began again.

"I can't believe this year's already almost over." Izzie sighed.

"I know, right? It feels like we just started our sophomore year, and here we are getting ready to take finals and become juniors. When my mom was still alive, I always heard my friends talk about how they couldn't wait to grow up. How everything was going by so slowly. I don't know about you, but I feel like it's racing by, and I kinda wish it would slow down."

Izzie let out a big sigh and squeezed Alison's hand. "I wish it would slow down too. I have so many questions, so many things I want to find out before life hits me square in the face. I don't know, I guess maybe I should just let it go, but like you said before, if it's important to me then I should chase it down. The only problem is, it's leading me nowhere. I keep seeing the same dreams and the same memories over and over, and nothing is connecting. I just don't understand."

"I don't know, Izzie. Maybe if you let up a little and let it run its course on its own you'll get the answers you're looking for. Sometimes, when we push for things, they push back. But when we let them grow in their own time, that's when we get the answers were looking for."

Izzie and Alison stopped at the edge of the forest, and Izzie hip-bumped her. "That was pretty deep, Alison, but I liked it, and it makes sense. I just hope I can let go enough to let it run its own course."

"And I wish I could take my own advice." Alison laughed, searching for any sign of the dragon's energy.

"I guess we're going to have to go into the forest and look for him. It's pretty much the perfect night for him to be out."

The girls clasped hands and started into the forest, stepping carefully over the fallen trees and through the wet leaves that covered the forest floor. When they reached the small cave where they had originally seen the dragon, they looked around. Suddenly a gust of air blew their hair, and Izzie watched the dragon glide between the trees and land in front of them.

Alison smiled at the soul in front of her. The colors were still just as wild as they had been inside the egg.

"So, I've learned some new things," the dragon said, still speaking like the girls.

"That's awesome, and holy *cow* have you gotten big," Izzie replied, shocked.

The dragon shrugged his scaled shoulders and dug his claws into the wet leaves beneath him. "Yeah, well, it's a pretty good place to catch game. I wouldn't say I'm overweight or anything like that, of course."

Izzie nodded, trying to hold back a smile. "No, of course not. You're the perfect weight."

The dragon shifted its stare to Alison and slowly walked toward her. "Hey, Alison. It's good to see you again. It gets lonely out here in the forest sometimes, but Horace hangs out with me, though I hate when he brings his mutt with him."

Alison smiled and shook her head, reaching out to pet the dragon. "I missed you too. Things have been crazy up at the school, especially with the Louper game and everything going on out in town. The whole thing is just a mess."

"I heard about the shifters." He turned his attention to Izzie. "I'm sorry about Luke, but he seemed to be playing okay in the game today."

"You were watching?"

"Of course, I was. I just had to stay back quite a bit so nobody would see me. Horace always freaks out when he finds me watching everybody, but I know what I'm doing. I won't get caught."

Alison laughed. "Yeah, that's what *we* said until we got caught coming out of the kemana. And, oh yeah, got caught bringing a dragon's egg into the bedroom, where he broke loose and completely tore the room apart."

He grimaced "Yeah, sorry about that...again. I mean, what can I say? I was just a baby."

Izzie wrinkled her nose and laughed. "I really hope that magical children are less destructive than dragon babies or I'm going to have to raise my child in a metal house."

Everyone laughed, and the dragon shook his head. "Don't worry. Usually, human babies don't have three-inch claws and sharp jagged teeth, so I think you'll be okay. Anyway, I learned a new trick. Do you want to see?"

Izzie nodded. "Of course we do."

The dragon straightened and lifted his head into the air, then breathed in quickly and blew a steady stream of frost into the girls' hair. He wasn't a fire-breathing dragon, after all. He was a frost-breathing dragon. Izzie and Alison giggled as they ran their fingers through their hair to dislodge the chunks of ice.

Izzie clapped her hands. "That's awesome!"

Alison was still picking ice out of her silver hair. "Okay, okay, how cold?"

Izzie looked around the ground kicking at the leaves until she found an old tennis ball that Horace's dog had chewed up. She held it out toward the dragon. He slowly approached and very carefully blew on it, breathing on the ball until it was frozen. Izzie looked at the frost that covered the once-yellow tennis ball. She squeezed it in her hand, and it shattered into a million pieces.

"Wow!" Izzie was stunned. She'd had never seen anything like that except on the weird science videos she had watched in middle school.

The dragon grinned, displaying his big teeth, and sat down, curling his tail around him. "So what's new with you girls? You have some kind of dance or something coming up?"

"Yeah, actually we do. We have this parent-and-student mixer coming up," Alison exclaimed excitedly. "It will be the first time that I've had a parent with me for anything since my mom died. My dad, James Brownstone, is flying in for it with Shay Carson, his girlfriend."

The dragon squealed like a teenage girl and slapped his tail against the ground. "I like the fact that you call Brownstone 'Dad' now. It's really nice to hear."

Izzie shrugged and kicked at the leaves. "It's cool and everything, but I don't have anybody coming to see me."

The dragon rubbed his face against her side. "Don't worry, Izzie. I don't have a family either, at least not parents. You and the girls are my family."

Alison felt a twinge of guilt run through her. She had been so excited to talk about her first experience with her dad at a dance that she'd completely forgotten about the fact that Izzie had no one in the world. Alison could be her best friend and even her sister, but she could never replace her mom and dad. Alison knew that all too well. While she called Brownstone Dad and she loved him very much, Shay and Brownstone would never truly replace the parents she'd had before everything got crazy. She didn't like Izzie being so sad. She rubbed her hands together and bit her lip figuring there was no reason that, as her sister, she couldn't have a good time with Brownstone as well.

"You know what, Izzie?" Alison began, putting her hand on Izzie's shoulder. "You don't have to be alone. Neither one of us have real parents here with us, but if Brownstone can be like a dad to me, then I'll share him with you so that you don't have to be alone. We'll go as a family to the dance. I couldn't ask for anything better than to have my sister by my side and share my new family with her."

A tear gathered in Izzie's eye, and she gave Alison a big hug. Sometimes, she didn't know if she deserved all the love Alison showed her, but she definitely wasn't going to turn it away.

25

James Brownstone stood in the foyer of the School of Necessary Magic. His black suit was tailored to fit his incredible muscles, and his tie was covered in pink flamingos, reminding him of their summer vacation. He stood back against the wall, smiling kindly at people as they passed. He noticed that they stared for a moment before hurrying by. He'd almost forgotten that the people there knew him as well as everybody else in the magical community, but he wasn't trying to make it awkward for anyone else. He already felt awkward enough on his own, not to mention that he was nervous as hell and trying to hide just how uncomfortable he was in a suit. It wasn't very often that he wore one, but for Alison, he was willing to make the sacrifice.

He tapped his foot and looked down at his watch as he waited for Alison and Izzie to put the finishing touches on their outfits. He was glad Alison had called him about Izzie. There was no way he'd turn down a girl with no family, and neither would Shay. Shay stood to the side, staring at the empty ROTC board and giggling. She walked back over to Brownstone, her heels clacking on the floor. Her black and pink dress fit snuggly and fell to right below the knees. She wore black stockings and tall black heels, making her quite a bit taller than she normally was. She looked at Brownstone and raised an eyebrow, smiling at him.

Brownstone grumbled and shook his head. "What are they doing up there? Never takes *you* that long to get ready."

"It's not like we go anywhere in fancy dresses and suits very often. It might take me a while too. And you've got to think Alison is super excited to see you, and Izzie is probably nervous as hell. Cut them some slack."

Alison and Izzie took each other's hands and squeezed tightly in excitement as they rounded the corner and stood at the top of the staircase. Izzie giggled when Brownstone shifted his stance and tugged on his tie before he noticed them standing there. Alison let out a deep breath of relief, taking comfort in sensing her dad's and Shay's energy. There was something about them that made it feel like home. The girls slowly made their way down the steps and stopped at the bottom, twirling to show their dresses off.

Shay's mouth rounded into an "O," and her eyes twinkled. She walked over and wrapped an arm around each girl.

"You girls look beautiful. Izzie, I love that shade of yellow on you, and the cut of that dress makes you look ten years older than you should. And Alison, you always look beautiful. I know you can't see the color, but that teal is absolutely perfect on you."

Shay backed up next to Brownstone, who cleared his throat and nodded at both the girls. She raised an eyebrow and elbowed him in the side, glancing down at the corsages he held in his big hands. They were small pink rosebuds, and they were gorgeous. Brownstone grabbed Alison's hand, kissing the back of it before sliding the corsage onto her wrist. She brought the flowers up to her nose and took in a deep breath before smiling and kissing Brownstone on the cheek. He blushed and turned to Izzie, nodding sweetly to her and repeating his actions.

"Thank you," Izzie whispered, taking a deep breath of the rosebuds.

Alison grabbed Shay's wrist, hugged her, and whispered into her ear, "Thank you so much for including Izzie."

"We are thrilled to do it. Thanks for giving us a heads-up," she whispered back.

"Well, ladies, are we ready to go into the dance?" Brownstone asked with a crooked smile.

Alison and Izzie each hooked an arm into one of Brownstone's, while Shay moved to the other side of Alison and did the same. The four of them walked through the doors of the cafeteria and Shay gasped, looking around the dining hall. It had been emptied of tables and chairs and decorated for the event. The ceiling had been enchanted to look like the Northern Lights, with its colors cascading across the ceiling. A huge red velvet rug was spread out as the dance floor, and beautiful gold and blue tapestries hung on the walls. The back wall looked like a waterfall, enchanted water cascading down into a bottomless pool.

Shay chuckled. "You magic people sure do know how to party."

Throughout the cafeteria, the students mingled with their parents. Some couples were just father and daughter, some groups had all three of them, and others were mothers and sons. The beautiful music coming from the stage wasn't the normal DJ. Instead, it was an orchestra made up of older witches and wizards dressed in tuxes and fancy dresses. Brownstone smiled at the ensemble and held out his hand toward Alison. She saw the energy swirling around him and smirked, nudging his hand toward Izzie.

"You go first."

Izzie smiled and squeezed Alison's hand before taking Brownstone's. He led her out onto the dance floor and Izzie placed one hand on his shoulder, the other was held in his. They danced around the room. Izzie closed her eyes as they moved, and lost herself in the music and the feeling of a fatherly figure dancing across the floor with her. For a moment, with her eyes still closed, a memory returned to her. She was dancing around the room, a room that looked like a large living room, and her small feet were on top of someone else's as he sang to her sweetly and twirled her around the room.

"Dad..." She whispered.

"What? I didn't hear you." Brownstone looked puzzled.

Izzie shook her head as the memory faded, trying to keep a happy look on her face. "It was nothing."

The memory had disappeared, but she could still feel herself clinging to the man in her memory as he swept her across the living room floor, humming the sweetest of tunes in her ear. She didn't know what to make of it. It was just another confusing piece of a very complicated puzzle. *Do I have a family? Why can't I remember?*

When Izzie and Brownstone were done dancing, it was Alison's turn to take a whirl. She danced with her father, clinging tightly to him as the music played loudly. Alison felt right at home with Brownstone's energy circulating around her, and the closeness of a father figure comforted her. Brownstone was surprised to find that he was happier than he had been in a very long time doing something so simple, which was just the way he liked it.

"Thank you for coming here," Alison whispered as they continue to dance. "It really means a lot to me that you're my dad and that you'd come to these things. It was hard, and I won't lie. It's still really hard sometimes, knowing not only that my mother is dead, but that my father is not my father anymore. When you adopted me though, that took most of that hurt away, and now I couldn't think of a better way to spend my night than dancing around this room with you."

Brownstone smiled and leaned his head against hers. "The only thing that would make it better? Some really good barbecue. I think that would make it perfect."

Alison laughed loudly as they took one more turn around the dance floor before making their way back to Izzie and Shay. The rest of the night was absolutely perfect for the both of them. The girls took turns dancing with Brownstone and chatted with Shay, making sure she knew that she was important as well.

"Aunt Shay, you remember Kathleen, Emma, Aya, Ethan, Luke, and Peter. These are my people, my family when I'm away from you guys. They've made my transition here so much smoother than I think it would've been without them."

"It's so nice to see you guys again. I've heard so much about you, and I want to thank you for being there for Alison. She's a special girl, and we love her very much."

Emma gave Shay a hug. "Thank you for making sure she came here. She really is an important part of this team, and I don't know what we'd do without her."

Brownstone walked up, and Alison introduced him to everyone as well. Izzie giggled as she watched Ethan and Peter stand tall and proud to try to impress the man that they had heard so many stories about. They had brave faces on, but Izzie knew better than that. Deep down inside, the man terrified them. About thirty minutes later, Tanner walked through the door. He'd promised Alison that he'd stop by, even though he didn't have any family to come with him to the party.

Alison squeezed Tanner's wrist and pulled him over in front of Brownstone and Shay. "And this is Tanner, one of my other very, very important friends. He came tonight just to meet you guys."

"It's nice to meet you. I've heard so much about you. Alison talks about you constantly."

Brownstone lifted an eyebrow but said nothing. He shook the boy's hand firmly. Alison slowly let out a breath of relief, glad that she hadn't just sprung on them that Tanner was her boyfriend. She figured that information could wait until later. Shay, on the other hand, gave him a wink as she leaned in and kissed him on the cheek. Brownstone might not have caught on, but Shay had guessed immediately. Luckily for Alison, Shay was quick to cover.

"Tanner… Yes, I remember that name. Brownstone, don't you remember me telling you that Alison was helping tutor a young man named Tanner?"

Brownstone nodded, but didn't really remember because Shay hadn't actually said it. He didn't want to admit it, figuring she had and he just hadn't heard her. "I… Yes, it's nice to meet you."

Izzie stood behind all of them, staring at the dance floor as Luke danced with his mother. She was also a shifter, a tall, slender, and elegant woman with a beautiful corsage on her wrist. Izzie didn't understand why Luke was avoiding her, and it was starting to infuriate her. So he had been poisoned and shifted without his control—Izzie understood. At first, she had tried to be understanding of the fact that he was embarrassed by it, but enough time had gone by. She was starting to lose her patience.

She turned back toward the group, trying to clear that from her head and diving in with her friends. Regardless of how upset she was, she was determined to have a good time.

W hen the weekend was over, the students trudged
back to their normal routines. They had several
classes every day that focused specifically on the
approaching end-of-year finals. Study Hall was busier than
it'd been all year, and even Ethan had found himself
dodging Leo Decker at all costs as he sat in the corner
reading all the material he had neglected throughout the
year. That morning, though, didn't start out quite like the
typical quiet morning would.

Chaos had erupted throughout the school, but it wasn't
because of some practical joke that Ethan had pulled or
even that dark magic spell that had injured one of the
students like the year before. Instead, it was subtle—something no one saw coming before they started walking
down the hallways. All the posters for the candidates for
class president and student body president were still on the
walls, and the photos continually moved. However, that
morning as the students stood around talking to each

other, they noticed something different about the speeches being given on the magic posters.

"My name is Scarlett, and I'm running for Student Body President. I want to tell you a secret about myself, something no one else knows. Late at night after everyone is in bed and I have sown fear through the students of this school, I burst into tears and cry myself to sleep in a puddle of saltwater and snot."

"Hello, School of Necessary Magic, my name is Wyatt. I'm running for Student Body President. I want to tell you a secret, something no one else knows. I use my father's money and clout to make people like me. They try to say it's because I'm a nice guy, but they know that's bullshit, and I don't mind it at all. I'd rather be liked for my money than have to put out the effort to make real friends."

"My name is Kathleen, and I'm running for Junior Class President. I'll tell you my secrets, but first I want to tell you a secret about this girl standing right here next to my poster."

The girl looked around and wondered if the poster was talking about her. She shrugged figuring there was no way it was just a trick. However, as Kathleen's animation continued, the student quickly realized it was not a trick at all.

"This girl's name is Annabelle Lace, and I know that she has a binder stuffed away in her dresser where she writes her name and Kyle Lovett's in with hearts and balloons. She dreams of a life where he loves her. The truth is, though...you have to come in close for this one because it's a really big secret."

The three people standing there looked at each other, then bent forward to hear the secret.

"Kyle Lovett is secretly in love with Professor Hudson."

Immediately, mayhem erupted in the halls. Everyone rushed back and forth, staying far enough away from the posters to keep their secrets but close enough to listen to the secrets about the candidates and others who stood too close. No one wanted to go to their next class, not when something that exciting was happening in the hallways. While some students broke down in tears, others laughed and pointed at the students mentioned, like Kyle Lovett. He didn't even know what was going on until he walked into the hall and everyone burst into laughter.

After about an hour, Professor Hudson walked around the corner and put her hands on her hips, trying to figure out what in the world had happened. She looked at the poster next to her as it blurted out one of her secrets. She ripped the poster from the wall and threw it in the trashcan, then walked down the hall casting a spell to silence all the posters. One by one, the animations froze, and the students scurried off to class.

Professor Fowler turned the corner, knowing exactly what was going on. She had come to help find whoever was responsible. While some found it hilarious, it had caused several students emotional distress, as well as started a couple of fights. She stood in the center of the hallway and closed her eyes, pulled energy up from the floor through her chest, and sent it out in a wave to illuminate the magic trail from the posters, but as she followed the glimmering footprints, they abruptly disappeared.

"Did you find them?" Professor Hudson asked.

"No, the trail just vanished. I don't even know where they would've gone unless they disappeared into thin air."

Professor Hudson crossed her arms and shook her head. "This is no student who pulled this off. The whole thing was way too clever, and the fact that their tracks disappear into thin air? Well, no student I know of would be able to hide as well as they can. Someone is causing trouble with dark intent, and we need to inform the head-mistress before it gets out of hand."

Professor Fowler agreed and rushed down the hall toward the headmistress' office. Professor Hudson stood there for a moment staring at the walls and wondered exactly who was trying to mess with the students. She already knew that they were not finished.

After their classes had finished and the students had stopped discussing the morning's incidents, they went to their dorms to prepare for the evening events. It was the night Izzie and all her friends had been waiting for, the premiere of *the Wizard of Oz*. Izzie stood backstage rubbing her hands together and peeked around the curtain. The place was packed. She closed the curtain and turned around with her eyes wide. She smoothed her hands down her blue-checked dress and walked over to the bike that was propped up against the wall.

Professor Fowler had enchanted a stuffed dog to walk and bark just like any other dog, except she'd spelled it to only follow the play's plot. It was a perfect way to include Toto without having to bring in an actual dog. The lights flickered in the house to quiet the audience, and butterflies fluttered in Izzie's stomach. She waited for the cue as they opened the heavy curtains to reveal the audience.

"Here goes nothing," Izzie whispered.

She threw herself into the play, remembered every line perfectly, and realized that she couldn't wait to perform the main song. She took a deep breath and closed her eyes as the music began to play. She had sung it a million times. She didn't think anything could ruin it for her...until she was about three lines in.

From somewhere out in the theater, she heard a voice echoing up onto the stage. "Aw, listen to the little orphan singing. Shouldn't this be *Little Orphan Annie* and not *Wizard of Oz*?"

Izzie cleared her throat between notes and shifted her stance, trying to ignore the heckler in the crowd, but it was becoming increasingly difficult. Several of the teachers walked the aisles to figure out who had yelled at the stage. However, every time they seemed to get close, the voice came from another direction. Alison, Kathleen, and the rest of her friends wanted badly to help her, but they had no idea how. She started to crumble under the pressure, and tears welled up in her eyes.

Scarlett, backstage at the edge of the curtain, watched as it unfolded. She gripped the curtain, thinking about the secrets the posters had shared that morning, then bit her lip, nodded, and did something very surprising. She took a deep breath, walked out on the stage, and came to Izzie's rescue. She didn't come out as Scarlett, but as Glinda the Good Witch, and waved her sparkly wand over the crowd to send shots of glitter over everyone's head. She swished the wand and sent a beam of light straight at the heckler, who froze with wide eyes as she gave him the death stare.

It was no secret that if you got the death stare from Scarlett, you'd better watch out. Every student in the place was pretty much terrified anytime Scarlett stared them down. The heckler nodded and leaned back in his seat, hunching so the teachers wouldn't find him. She curtsied at the crowd, swirled her wand around Izzie, and gave her a wink.

"Sometimes, you'll find there's more than one bad witch in the crowd, but fortunately for you, this one was pretty easy to take care of," Scarlett said in character, smiling and batting her eyelashes.

The crowd clapped as Scarlett bowed and flitted off the stage, leaving Izzie to sing her big song. Before she exited she squeezed Izzie's hand and nodded, letting her know that everything would be okay. Out in the seats, Kathleen leaned toward Alison and cupped her hand over her mouth.

"Who knew? I guess even Scarlett can do the right thing once in a while."

Alison smiled and nodded. "I had a feeling that Scarlett had it in her, but I won't get my hopes up for the future."

With a renewed sense of confidence, Izzie walked to the front of the stage and belted out the rest of the song. By the time she finished the last note, there wasn't a dry eye in the house. There was a momentary pause when she finished the song before the entire audience got to their feet and gave her a roaring ovation. She smiled and winked at her friends, then continued the scene. The play had turned out even better than she'd imagined, and especially so because she'd had Scarlett by her side. She didn't know what made Scarlett tick, but that was okay.

27

It was June, and very hot outside in Charlottesville, Virginia. The loud chittering of cicadas echoed across the green fields, and the trees were dense and thick. Lines of students slowly trundled across the courtyard and into the foyer of the mansion. Those standing outside used the different candidates' flyers to fan themselves, but this time the students running for office had decided not to enchant them. They didn't want to chance revealing any more secrets. The students talked excitedly as they waited for their chance to magically vote and feed it into a virtual screen that was tallying the totals for the elections in real time.

"Who are you voting for?" one of the students asked her friends.

"I'm not telling. I think it's important that everyone have the opportunity to vote exactly how they want to without being bullied, pushed, or peer-pressured, for that matter, into voting for the most popular."

The girl shrugged and took a sip of her water. "I'm

voting for Scarlett, and I'm not afraid to tell everybody. And before you ask, no, I'm not voting for her because I'm afraid of her. I'm voting for her because I think deep down she's a good person, and she showed it during the play. Everyone tried to play it off like they didn't know what she was doing, but she was saving Izzie from that terrible heckler. I think that shows a lot of character."

Her friend rolled her eyes. "And this is the generation of voters to come."

The professors meandered around the courtyard, maintaining order and handing out water so that nobody got dehydrated. Clusters of people stood watching the board as the numbers changed, anxious to see who was winning. Most of the votes for student body president went to Scarlett and Wyatt, but a few also went to Farrell. Most of those came from shifters who hadn't found any friends. They didn't know what Farrell stood for but felt most comfortable with somebody who was like them in office. He had gotten their attention with his bravery, which was exactly what he was looking for, but he had never expected to win. He was, however, grateful that he hadn't gone out with zero votes.

Scarlett stood at the bottom of the steps leading up into the mansion with a platter of cookies and handed them out as people entered. Wyatt looked at her and rolled his eyes, but she just laughed.

"All's fair…"

The voting took several hours, and as soon as the last vote had been entered the results popped up on the screen. Scarlett had managed to beat Wyatt by just a handful of votes. She was the winner, and she wasn't afraid to show it.

She pranced around hugging her friends and waved like a beauty queen to everyone in the courtyard. A couple of people cheered and jumped up and down, excited that Scarlett had won. The rest of them were just relieved, knowing they wouldn't have to feel harassed until the end of the year. Wyatt was bummed but let it go, figuring he didn't really have enough time to do the job anyway. He was going to make sure he was on the Louper team the next year too, and since it would be his senior year, he wanted to give everything he had to the sport.

Ethan elbowed Peter and whispered, "Buckle up. Next year is going to be a bumpy ride!"

The whole school was in a celebratory mood, with just a few stragglers running around clutching their books to their chests as they tried to finish the last few exams. They were in the final countdown to the end of the year and summer. The professors allowed the students to mill around the grounds and walk through the mansion talking about the excitement of the elections that day. They had all worked hard that year, and the headmistress didn't want to spoil the fun by forcing them to return to their dorm rooms.

Scarlett stood in the center of the foyer, and Izzie was talking to Kathleen about five feet away. Scarlett put her hands to her chest and dramatically leaned her head back, smiling and closing her eyes.

"I'm so excited that I won. This is even better than if I had gotten to play Dorothy."

Kathleen rolled her eyes, and Izzie smiled, shaking her head. "Let it go. She's right—this is bigger. I think it all worked out in the end."

"I suppose you're right." Kathleen smiled. "This year has definitely been crazy, I'm not gonna lie about that. So many ups and downs! I really hope our junior year goes a little bit more smoothly. And of course it should, since I'll be president of our class."

Izzie nodded, spotting Luke across the foyer. "I'm sure it will. If you'll excuse me, though, there's something I need to take care of."

Kathleen lifted an eyebrow and looked at Luke, then nodded and patted Izzie on the shoulder. Izzie wasn't going to let him avoid her anymore. She was tired of it. She hurried across the entryway, grabbed him by the arm, and pulled him into the corner away from the rest of the students. He backed up into the wall, Izzie in front of him with her hands on her hips and an angry look on her face.

"You're not getting away from me this time, not until we have a talk. I don't understand what happened, Luke. I like you, and I thought you liked me too. I mean, you made it seem like that for the entire first half of the year. I personally don't go around just kissing anyone, randomly holding hands, taking them to dances, or any of those things unless I actually like them."

Luke blinked and shook his head, looking completely confused. "I don't understand. How can you still like me after what happened?"

"What?" Izzie was taken aback. "What happened wasn't your fault. There is nothing wrong with you being a shifter. I thought I made it very clear from the first moment I met you. You're different, not wrong. We're all different. I blew a hole in the potions classroom wall this year while tripping on some strange herbs that my professor picked on another planet. I'm pretty sure that's just as weird."

Luke chuckled, trying to hide his smile. He had almost forgotten Izzie had done that, even though the charred cement blocks were still visible on the outside of the mansion. Izzie let out a deep breath and grasped his hand.

"Look, Luke, I know you went through a lot this year. I really do, but we all did. And we can't just give up on the things that are most important to us because we're afraid of how the other person will react. By now, I should hope you would know that there isn't much that could make me not like you. Not unless you became some crazy dark-magic shifter-wizard and tried to kill me or something."

Luke chuckled and shook his head. "I really don't see that happening. I'm so sorry, Izzie. I didn't mean to hurt your feelings. I do like you. Actually, I like you very much, and I don't want to lose that."

Izzie smiled and squeezed his hand. "Then stop being such a dork, and let's go get some food. I heard that instead of having magical plates today, they just set up a huge buffet of food and drinks to make things easier for the kitchen staff. Apparently, there's pretty much everything you could ever want on this buffet. I'm dead serious."

Luke laughed and squeezed her hand back. "Will do. So, what are we waiting for?"

The staff was trying something different this year and had filled the dining hall full of food to celebrate another year gone by. There were cakes, dips, sandwiches, burgers, hot dogs, pasta dishes, and everything else you could possibly think of. It had seemed like the perfect idea—an easy buffet that could sit there all day for anybody who was hungry. However, they quickly realized that something wasn't right.

After everyone had had at least one plate, different areas of the cafeteria started going quiet. Groups of people backed into the center of the room, realizing that it was happening again, only this time it was much worse. Every shifter at the school had been poisoned, but this time there wasn't enough time to get out the door and go into the woods. The teachers formed a protective ring around the students in the center. Around the edges of the room and right in front of them, the shifters changed into wolves. They shredded their clothes, then turned to face the roomful of students and teachers.

The teachers held their arms out protecting the students as well as they could while trying to remember that people were against the walls as well, and that included a couple of professors too. They reminded everyone that the students were the same as always, just furrier. The shifters growled and pawed at the floor, which didn't help. Everyone was terrified, not being used to shifters in wolf form although intellectually they knew they were the same. Shrieks echoed out the doors and across the courtyard.

Headmistress Berens barreled through the cafeteria doors with her wand high. Alison ran in behind her and scanned the area for souls. She found a large group of magical beings huddled together, while the shifters' energy surrounded them.

The headmistress swished her wand at the students in the center, sending a burst of energy out that pushed them against the walls. Alison closed her eyes and created a shadow that threw darkness over the room, giving the wolves a chance to escape. As Alison stood there in the darkness, she felt fur brush her arms and legs as the wolves dashed for the doors and safety.

As soon as the darkness lifted, Izzie raced toward the door. The headmistress tried to stop her, but she was too late. Izzie disappeared around the corner, running as fast as she could to catch up with Luke. She pulled energy into her palm and sent it spiraling out over the field. She was using it to track them, not letting it go this time even though she knew the wolves could easily outrun her. She had given up on Luke the first time, but she would never do that again.

Before she made it to the hill, one of the wolves turned back and skidded to a stop right in front of her. His large head hovered at the height of her face, his whiskers glistened in the sunlight, and his amber eyes were all too familiar. Unafraid, Izzie rubbed her hand across his head, feeling the softness of his fur between her fingers. She didn't flinch when his sharp fangs hovered near her nose. She stared into his eyes for several moments before she smiled.

"I love you, Luke."

The wolf's eyes grew large, and he reared back. His head lifted into the air as he let out a deep howl that echoed around them. He nodded at Izzie, then turned and loped away. As he crested the hill, he stopped one last time and looked back at Izzie, who stood there waving at him with a smile on her face. His eyes glistened as he turned and picked up speed, running to catch up with the pack. Izzie stood there long after he had disappeared into the woods with her heart beating wildly in her chest. She didn't know why it had taken her so long to tell Luke how she felt. She wasn't sure she had even known until that moment, but it was the perfect end to a very confusing day.

28

Early the next morning, as the sun rose over the hills, the shifters quietly returned to the school grounds and found their clothes at the edge of the woods, where the headmistress had directed them to be left in neat piles. She had called everyone into the cafeteria afterward to explain to the students what had happened. She knew that word was going to get out, and she wanted them to understand that they didn't need to fear the shifters. Everything had been under control. The shifters had just been scared when they'd turned into their wolves without control because someone had poisoned them.

As the shifters dressed, Headmistress Berens called all the professors into the meeting room, including Professor Hodges, who had no idea what had happened. They weren't as nervous as they had been the first time, but only because they had seen it once before. It wasn't a surprise that someone had struck again, especially after the issue with the posters.

"I still don't understand. What happened to the shifters last night?" Professor Hodges asked, shaking his head. His hair was a mess, which was not like him at all.

Professor Powell tapped his fingers on the desk. "I do. I know exactly what happened. It was the lemonade. I went back into the buffet and did a spell to try to figure out what had been poisoned. It was perfectly harmless to anyone else, but there was a strange compound in it. Something new. Whatever it is, when a shifter consumes it, it triggers something inside of them that forces them to shift into their wolves."

Professor Hudson removed her glasses and wiped the lenses with a tissue. "I don't understand. They're creating new compounds?"

Professor Powell shook his head. "It's not necessarily new, as in 'just created,' just new as in I have never seen it before. Personally, I think it's something old, dark magic that we haven't seen in centuries."

One of the teachers gasped. "Someone is trying to close the school. They're trying to create fear in everyone, including the dark families who bring their children here. Whoever this person is, they are not going to stop until they get their way."

Everyone began to talk, but the headmistress put up her hand. "It's not some*one*. It's a group—some of the dark families who want to gain power, not give it away. I can't imagine it was any of the parents who sent their children here since I met with each and every one of them, but there are so many dark families out there. So many we haven't even met yet, hiding in the shadows and waiting for an opportunity. They see us as a threat, and they're not going to stop. We're going to have to be ready for them in the fall."

The headmistress had wanted to put out a statement letting the parents know what had happened, but since it was so close to when the students were getting picked up, she didn't have a chance to. Most of the parents, however, had already heard about it. When they arrived at the school, they were in a tizzy. They were terrified that the shifters had hurt their children, the dark families were trying to take over, or that something even fouler was in play.

As the parents began to arrive, the headmistress made sure that she was available to speak to every parent who had concerns. She didn't want the children to be withdrawn from the school because of this, but she understood that there was not a lot that she could do, especially since they didn't have any answers. However, she was able to calm most of them down with the help of Professor Hudson and Professor Powell, who went through the security that they would be implementing before the children returned in the fall.

It wasn't even technically the day to pick up the kids yet, but after word spread some of the parents had made haste, opening portals, jumping on planes, or taking the magic train to Charlottesville to pick up their children. A lot of the dark wizard families who had enrolled their students were the first to arrive. Some were outraged that they had shifters changing in the school like that, while others wanted to tell the headmistress that they'd had nothing to do with what had happened.

"I fully understand your concerns," Headmistress Berens assured one of the dark magic families. "You trusted that we would take care of your child, but to be fair, no one was injured during this occurrence. No one except the shifters."

"We are trying to be understanding," the mother said, holding her child close. "We also want you to know that our family had nothing to do with this. We cannot speak for the others, but we can speak for ours. As soon as it happened, we called a meeting and made sure that nothing had slipped through the cracks. We might be part of the dark families, but we are not part of the family that has caused all these problems recently. We will see how things go, and make a decision on the fall. We will let you know."

By the time the last of the families had collected their children, the headmistress was exhausted. She had repeated herself a hundred times, and she knew she'd have to repeat herself a hundred times more before all the students were picked up. There were also magical beings out there who hadn't yet heard about what had happened, and she would have to approach the subject carefully with them when they came for their children. She didn't want them to hear it from the kids. It would be better if it came from her. She really had no control over the situation, but she hoped for the best.

Down in the foyer, Izzie and the others stood talking

and saying goodbye to the other students who were already leaving. Izzie leaned against the railing looking out over the crowd of people and wondered where Luke was. They'd all returned that morning, but she assumed that he needed a while to collect himself. Without her realizing it, Luke snuck up behind her and grabbed her hand, pulling her with him. They moved down the hallway to the conference room and closed the door behind them.

Luke ran his hands over Izzie's face and looked deep into her eyes as he leaned in and kissed her. She smiled, her hands pressed against his warm body, happy to feel him close again and more than happy to know he was safe. He pulled back, smiling.

"Thank you. You weren't afraid of me at all."

"What was there to be afraid of?" she asked, smiling back. "I know you. I know those eyes, and I know that you would never hurt me."

He smirked and kissed her again, running his hand gently through her hair. "I'm going to visit you here over the summer if the headmistress will allow me to. And you —you can come visit me anytime you want to. My father knows about you, and you are always welcome in our home. I don't want to go the whole summer without seeing you. To be quite honest, I don't want to go a day without talking to you."

Izzie smiled, not believing how everything had turned out. The year had started off slowly, but by the time it ended, she had Luke in her arms and a warm feeling in her heart, and she had accomplished much that year even if none of it had to do with her past. She already couldn't wait until the next year started so that she could be back with her friends and with Luke by her side.

"Our junior year is gonna be amazing." Luke smiled.

"I have a feeling there are going to be a few vacancies next year," she stated, laughing. "It's a school for magical teenagers, and they're thrown off by a little chaos? Life is not going to be easy for them in the future."

They laughed, hugged each other tightly, and kissed one last time before they left the room. Izzie knew he was right, though. Next year was *definitely* going to be amazing.

The whole crew rode the jitney and got off at the Starbucks in town. They nonchalantly walked past the counter and down the hall, following the line of other students through the magical wall and out onto the landing. Slowly, they moved down the steps as they talked loudly about their summer plans and exchanged goodbyes, knowing that their trains would be there soon.

Izzie looked up as the woman's voice came over the loudspeaker announcing the train. "Red Line with stops from New York to San Francisco is boarding. Please have your pass ready when you board the train and take a seat in the first available place."

"Dang, that's my train," Alison replied, grabbing Izzie's hand and hurrying down the steps toward the platform two stories below.

When they got to the bottom, Alison quickly turned and hugged Izzie tightly. "I promise I'll text you. I'll call you. We'll *have* to see each other this summer. I don't want to go all summer without it."

Izzie hugged her back and nodded, watching as Alison easily maneuvered through the crowd toward the train. She still couldn't believe how well Alison made her way around. She had been right from the beginning—just give her some space, and no one would know that she couldn't see. Izzie was constantly in awe of the strength and wonder of her best friend.

"Well, kid, it was a pretty good year."

Izzie turned away from the train and looked at the next landing up, from which Scarlett smiled down at her.

"Yeah, it was."

Scarlett came down the steps and stood in front of her with her hand up. "Don't get the wrong idea. You and me, we're not buddies, but I respect you. You're pretty tough. I like that. Wolf boyfriend and all."

Izzie shrugged, figuring she would take that. It was better than her picking on her any day. "I'll see you in the fall, Scarlett."

Scarlett began to walk away but turned back to her. "That's 'Madam President,' and yes, you will."

Izzie chuckled as Scarlett headed toward the train. She walked up and stood on the landing, leaning over the railing and watching as everyone streamed past her. The last time she had stood there, her thoughts had been all over the place, but this time it was a little bit simpler. She realized that she had a lot of people in her life who really cared about her. Those people were the ones who were going to be constantly on her mind throughout the summer, helping her get through the loneliness until school started again in the fall. A warm feeling settled into her chest and she sighed, letting a smile move across her lips. She planned to figure out who those people in her flashes of memories and dreams were, but she no longer wallowed in misery. A family was what you made it, not who you were given, and she had one hell of a family right there at her school.

I'm working off of a new philosophy these days. *If I don't see a problem, there is no problem.* I know, I know, a little background is needed. Otherwise, it sounds like I'm looking away from the wreckage. Nope. It's actually having the opposite effect.

I should point out that I'm sitting in a rental pad that's a small bachelor pad (3-foot Budweiser neon sign on the wall, black leather couches, big fish tank on the wall – with no fish, and the TV remotes that are rubber-banded together are fancier than I can manage), sleeping on the couch because the bed is at my chest level. (It took hoisting up a leg and using my head as leverage to roll into it. Lois Lane, the good dog who can leap a couch without hesitation gave it a try but couldn't do it.)

Just about everything I own is in storage right now – one house is sold and the other isn't quite finished yet – and this is the 2nd place I've moved into so far. The first was a hotel but I only lasted two weeks before I went searching for a better solution.

Bottom line for me is that I had to decide pretty quickly if I wanted to see what I didn't like about all of this or look for the opportunities.

If your routine and 95 percent of what you own was stripped away, and you were in a new neighborhood, what would you suddenly see about yourself?

The willingness to even look was key. Frankly, all the things that I don't have temporarily were what I used to ignore the mild irritations of life. Oh, and by the way I started eating healthy about three months ago, so fat and sugar aren't hanging around to help out either.

I put the pedal to the metal of self-realization, not entirely on purpose but once I saw it, I dove in further, head first.

Here's what I got out of it. I'm lonely.

I'm an author so you can figure I like being alone and I have a lot of friends that I adore hanging out with all the time. But in this empty space with so few distractions I got that a lot of the time I'm relating an exciting life to others instead of sharing it with someone special.

That was Part A. Part B was looking at all the clever ways I've managed to ignore that feeling and to stay alone. Working 24/7 is one way that comes to mind. Telling myself, I can do it – that's more efficient anyway, is another. There's a list of them.

Okay, back to the new motto. I don't have to see all of this as a problem. That brings on shame (a useless feeling) and only slows down change. Instead, I see it as the consequences of my past behavior and I'm going with acceptance. In other words, *data*. If I don't like the consequences, I can change it. Moving is actually part of that, and so is eating better. There are other changes I'm making like bringing on the wonderful Felicia B as my new virtual assistant to help me get more done and have more time.

There's an element of trust mixed in now also that I also think I lacked before – I didn't want to find out I couldn't find someone to take on this wild, wonderful life with me. Fuck that idea, I got this...

My time as a wandering nomad is coming to an end in a couple of weeks and I'll be in that new house. But, I'm taking with me this new awareness and I'm heading out there. More adventures to follow.

Author Notes – Standing in for Michael Anderle is his son (middle) Jacob

Howdy, folks, it's the middle son writing. For most of y'all I haven't been on the radar, since unlike my brothers, I do not write professionally or otherwise. However, *like* my brothers I have been with my dad throughout his writing escapades, from meager beginnings to going all around the world for conventions. My father has had many forks in the road, as well as breaks in his career.

The subject of this one is simply a slice of life, as it were.

It was a slightly chilly winter morning near our home in Dallas-Fort Worth, and the sun had been in the sky for only a couple of hours when Dad, Joey and I went to one of our haunts: Bottlecap Alley Icehouse Grill. When we got out of the car, the three of us were in a jovial mood.

Good food and our regular spot were waiting inside. What wasn't great about that?

After ordering our breakfasts (or rather, early lunches), the three of us sat down at the corner table and chatted like we normally do, Joey and Dad joking back and forth while I listened.

At some point during the conversation, my father took out his laptop. For some, it may be strange for a man to pull out a laptop in the middle of a conversation with his sons. However, since his businesses were on the net, most of the time when we saw him he was clutching some form of technology—and vice versa. We didn't mind.

This sparked a question from the two of us. For the past three months (this was December 2015), Joey and I had been interested in how our dad's books were doing. "Hey, Papa," asks we, "how are the books coming along?"

Dad looked up from the screen and a smile graced his features as he started to tip-tap his way toward a website. "Y'all both know I've been having better and better days, right?"

Joey and I nodded.

Turning his laptop around, Dad presented his newest figures from Amazon. Joey and I gasped in surprise. "Dad, you passed the hundred mark!"

My dad laughed and beamed about the accomplishment. At the time of this memory, my father had published the third book, so his sales were starting to rise.

When we looked at the graph, it hadn't been his first jump. There were some dips back to the double digits, but when Joey and I saw the new average, I remember it being in the lower hundreds in income per day.

All three of us were excited about the achievement. It was the one of many Joey and I experienced with Dad during his humble start in publishing. This memory about my father, Michael Anderle, is one of my favorites about his pursuit of authorhood.

Since we saw his ratings from day one, I know it didn't happen overnight.

This was just one of many stories I can remember. My dad may not need any lessons in humility when he reads these *Notes*, but by looking at the past, we all can learn a little something.

Or have a memory resurface.

Jacob Anderle

- Rule of Magic (4) - Dealing in Magic (5) - Theft of Magic (6) -
Enemies of Magic (7) - Guardians of Magic (8)

The Soul Stone Mage Series

* Sarah Noffke and Martha Carr *

House of Enchanted (1) - The Dark Forest (2) - Mountain of
Truth (3) - Land of Terran (4) - New Egypt (5) - Lancothy (6) -
Virgo (7)

The Kacy Chronicles

* A.L. Knorr and Martha Carr *

Descendant (1) - Ascendant (2) - Combatant (3) - Transcendent
(4)

The Midwest Magic Chronicles

* Flint Maxwell and Martha Carr*

The Midwest Witch (1) - The Midwest Wanderer (2) - The
Midwest Whisperer (3) - The Midwest War (4)

The Fairhaven Chronicles

* with S.M. Boyce *

Glow (1) - Shimmer (2) - Ember (3) - Nightfall (4)

CONNECT WITH THE AUTHORS

Martha Carr Social

Website: http://www.marthacarr.com

Facebook: https://www.facebook.com/
groups/MarthaCarrFans/

Michael Anderle Social

Website: http://kurtherianbooks.com/

Email List: http://kurtherianbooks.com/email-list/

Facebook Here: https://www.
facebook.com/TheKurtherianGambitBooks/